RABBI EIZIK

Also by ANDREW HANDLER:

The Zirids of Granada

Ararát: A Collection of Hungarian-Jewish Short Stories
(Translated from the Hungarian with an Introduction and
Notes)

RABBI EIZIK

Hasidic Stories
about the Zaddik of Kálló

Translated from the Hungarian
with an Introduction and Notes by

ANDREW HANDLER

Rutherford • Madison • Teaneck
Fairleigh Dickinson University Press
London: Associated University Presses

© 1978 by Associated University Presses, Inc.

Associated University Presses, Inc.
Cranbury, New Jersey 08512

Associated University Presses
Magdalen House
136–148 Tooley Street
London SE1 2TT, England

Main entry under title:
                    Rabbi Eizik
Bibliography: p.
CONTENTS: Neumann, A. The Rebbe's song.—Patai, J.
The singing saint.—Neumann, A. The miraculous recovery. [etc.]
1. Tales, Hasidic. 2. Taub Eizik, 1751–1821—Legends. 3.
Jews in Nagykálló, Hungary—Literary collections. I. Handler,
Andrew, 1935–   II. Neumann, Albert, d. 1943. III. Szabolcsi,
Lajos, IV. Patai, József, 1882–1953.
      PM532. R28   894'.511'3008   75–5245
                    ISBN 0–8386–1739–5

PRINTED IN THE UNITED STATES OF AMERICA

Contents

Introduction

The Turkish occupation of Hungary, which ended with the Peace of Karlowitz in 1699, left behind an unhappy people and a ravaged land. For 150 years Hungary had been a main battlefield for the armies of the Hapsburg emperors and the Turkish sultans. Finally, the imperial troops, under the able leadership of Prince Eugene of Savoy, decisively defeated a large Turkish force and put an end to the last Muslim attempt for the conquest of Christian Europe. The aftermath of the Turkish occupation was predictable. Hungary lay in ruins, and its population, which had been drastically reduced in number, showed the unmistakable signs of exhaustion and lethargy. Once again Hungary became a possession of the Hapsburgs, and the returning imperial administrators wasted little time in making plans for the reestablishment of law and order and for social and economic recovery. Their efforts, however, proved unsuccessful. The traditional heavy-handedness of Hapsburg absolutism, the increasingly widening socioeconomic gap between peasants and nobles, the attacks of marauding groups of soldiers on villages, farms, and traveling individuals, and the virtually unchecked power of regional military commanders hindered the work of rebuilding. The prevailing difficulties further increased due to the confusion that accompanied the influx of newcomers—Rumanians, Croats, Serbs, Slovaks, and Ukranians—who settled on large tracts of empty or abandoned land at the encouragement of the imperial government.

7

The general dissatisfaction with the unremedied social and economic conditions exploded in the form of a sweeping anti-Hapsburg uprising (1703–1711). Led by Ferenc Rákóczi II, (1676–1735), the wealthiest landowner in Hungary, whose stepfather, Imre Thököly (1657–1705) had been the leader of an earlier uprising against the Hapsburgs, the ever-increasing forces of Hungarian soldiers won a number of victories at the outset. Its high point was the Parliament of Ónod (1707) which severed all national ties of allegiance to the Hapsburgs and declared the independence of Hungary. The Rákóczi revolt, however, was doomed to failure by the very nature of the men supporting it and by the lack of support it received from anti-Hapsburg foreign powers. Rivalry among peasant leaders and aristocratic generals resulted in uncoordinated and faulty military planning that failed to transform brilliantly fought battles into a sustained drive to final victory, and the failure of the French and Turkish governments to render effective support despite earlier pledges of military cooperation led to the collapse of Rákóczi's independent Hungary.

One tangible result of the revolt was the noticeable change in the attitude of the returning Hapsburg administration. It became apparent that the traditional methods of brutal absolutism had failed to achieve their objective. The cooperation of Hungarians could be won only with gestures of leniency and a benevolent government. For nearly 150 years, Hapsburg rule in Hungary was not challenged effectively.

The resumption of the work of rebuilding, however, did not succeed in setting the expected pace of progress. Throughout the eighteenth century, the social and economic objectives of the imperial government differed significantly from what the Hungarians expected to achieve. The introduction of mercantilism and the encouragement of commercial and industrial development satisfied the Hungarians only in principle. The new influx of foreign settlers from the 1720s, the growing competition between Austrian and Hungarian traders and manufacturers, the failure of the imperial government to remove the countless medieval restrictions that greatly hampered the development of a progressive system of international trade, the appearance of a large number of foreign merchants from the 1730s, and the gradual sinking of the Hungarian peasants into semiserfdom on the estates of absentee landowners were the signs of sobering reality that reconfirmed the Hungarians' conviction that, despite the absence of heavy-handed techniques of suppression, the Hapsburgs envisaged for Hungary a role no better than that of a subservient vassal in their multinational empire. Lacking the means for rekindling the fire of open revolt, the opposition to Hapsburg imperialism was forced to adopt the weapons of implicit, nonviolent resistance. Encouraged by the sweeping ideas of the Age of Enlightenment, Hungarian intellectuals initiated the detailed and scientific study of the Hungarian language which, in time, was to become the vehicle of a new national cultural movement. Their effort was successful. It survived the enlightened but uncompromisingly Germanizing rule of Joseph II (1780–90), the shock caused by the execution of Hungarian Jacobinist leaders in 1795, the repercussions of the French Revolution and the Age of Napoleon in the Hapsburg empire, and the Metternich era. The Revolution of 1848 and the Compromise of 1867, which overhauled the empire and give the Hungarians near equality in the new partnership arrangement, were the long-range objectives that the cultural movement, later augmented by powerful political leadership, helped to achieve.

Within the national confines, the history of the Jews in Hungary shows similar signs of turbulance, readjustment, struggle, and achievement. The end of the Turkish occupation, however, meant the beginning of a new era for them. Although there was little change in the attitude of the Church and the cities, both being strongholds of anti-Jewish sentiment, the prevailing conditions favored increasing, yet

carefully circumscribed, participation of the Jews in the task
of rebuilding the economic and social foundations of Hungary.
The Hapsburg policy of encouraging the immigration of a
large number of foreign settlers had a favorable effect on
the Jewish communities of Hungary, which had been showing
signs of significant numerical decline. The influx of Austrian
and German Jews was followed by the settlement of Moravian
and Bohemian Jews. The largest group of Jewish immigrants,
however, arrived from Poland. Frightened by the ferocity
of the Chmielniczki uprising (1648), by the upsurge of ritual
murder accusations, and by the gradual disappearance of the
last vestiges of central authority, a large number of Polish
Jews took advantage of the First Partitioning of Poland in
1772, by which Galicia came under the rule of the Hapsburgs,
and sought permission to resettle in those parts of the empire,
such as Hungary, which were the most adversely affected
by the long Turkish occupation and were the most likely
to offer them security and opportunity in the task of rebuilding. The integration of the newcomers into Hungarian society,
however, fell short of their expectations. Jews—long-time
residents and recent immigrants alike—were forbidden by
the virtually independent municipal governments, powerfully
supported by exclusivist guilds, to settle in the cities. Those
few who received permission for a temporary, short-term stay
were heavily taxed. Considerably better treatment awaited
them on the estates and in the towns owned by wealthy
Hungarian nobles. Unlike in the cities, where Jews were
viewed as undesirable and dangerous commercial competitors,
the estates of the nobles provided them security and opportunity. Although most nobles undoubtedly regarded their
Jewish tenants merely as profitably taxable subjects, there
were some who had synagogues built for them or who
donated parcels of land for them to build on. It was on the
domains of the nobles that the vast majority of the Jews in
Hungary gained a strong foothold. They were provided with
the opportunity to engage in the cultivation of land, the

raising of cattle, trade, and a variety of other occupations, and to initiate their enduring struggle for settlement in the proudly autonomous royal cities.

Although Hungarian, Austrian, and foreign merchants became increasingly active after the collapse of the Rákóczi revolt, Jews distinguished themselves in the economic recovery of Hungary. One eighteenth-century writer, Count Szapáry, described them as the most important men of trade. They were also engaged in numerous branches of export-import trade, which took them to all regions of the empire.

The reign of Joseph II was a turning point in the history of the Jews in Hungary. The enlightened monarch's sweeping reforms included carefully detailed instructions that broke through the enduring restrictions of a medieval tradition. The *Systematica gentis judaicae regulatio* (1783) gave the Jews permission to settle in all cities of the empire, except in mining towns, thereby curbing one of the most jealously guarded municipal privileges of virtual self-government. It also gave them the right to secular education, even at the universities, and to unrestricted participation in all branches of economic activity.

Joseph's death in 1790 ended the short period of enlightened government. Although most of his reforms did not survive him, the position of the Jews in Hungary was not affected so adversely as might have been expected. The gradual emergence of a Jewish middle class and the impact of secularism that the Age of Enlightenment had fostered, paved the way toward slow integration into the society of Christian Hungary. The process of Magyarization and the emergent feeling of strong patriotism became the characteristic features of the Jews of Hungary. Their quest for social acceptance, however, was only grudgingly tolerated and often resisted. Most Jews, to be sure, failed to meet the standards of social integration. They remained strict, exclusivist traditionalists and upheld rabbinical leadership. Yet the number of those who spoke Hungarian, dressed in contemporary fashion, and supported revolutionary activities continued to grow. Jewish participation in the Hungarian Revolution of 1848, however, far outstripped all expectations. A large number of Jews volunteered for service in the revolutionary armies and distinguished themselves on the battlefields. The granting of citizenship for the Jews in Hungary in 1867 was a belated sign of appreciation.

One notable feature of each of the three consecutive waves of Jewish immigration into Hungary was the infusion of prevailing regional trends. The Austrian-German Jews brought the spirit of absolutism and strict conservatism into communal life. The Moravian-Bohemian Jews, who were the pioneers of secularism and reform, championed the cause of social assimilation. The Polish Jews planted the seeds in Hungary of the movement that, from the middle of the eighteenth century had swept over the Jewish communities of Poland and Lithuania, namely Hasidism. The development of Hasidism in Hungary, however, was markedly different in both circumstance and nature from the evolution of the movement. In Poland particular circumstances, such as the turbulent aftermath of the Chmielniczki massacres, the widespread feeling of insecurity and fear created by the steady deterioration of central government, and the deep sense of disillusionment that followed the tragic course of the Sabbatian and Frankist movements, created a uniquely blended religious and psychological gap that Hasidism, with its ideals of personal relationship between the individual and God and escape from the strict confines of rabbinical control, succeeded in filling. No such circumstances were evident in Hungary in the seventeenth and eighteenth centuries. The Jewish share of suffering during the Turkish occupation and the Rákóczi revolt was not noticeably greater than that of the vast majority of non-Jewish Hungarians. The restoration of Hapsburg absolutism meant the revival of strong central authority, which the Hungarians were unable to challenge effectively until 1848. Although both the Sabbatians and the Frankists had hoped to recruit followers in Hungary, neither movement achieved the mass support it had found in Poland and Lithuania. The heterogeneous composition of Hungarian Jewry and their growing feeling of patriotism effectively cushioned them against the impact of foreign influence. Furthermore, Hasidism in Hungary was by no means a nationwide movement. For a long time it was restricted to the northeastern regions. In its initial stages no sharp lines of demarkation were drawn between its followers and those who adhered to rabbinical leadership, and the two groups were often indistinguishably fused. The religious sensitivities of the traditionalists were dulled by the lack of unified leadership and other priorities. The Chief Rabbinate of Hungary was abolished in 1753, before the appearance of the earliest organized and recognizable hasidic group. Influential orthodox rabbis, such as Moses Sofer of Bratislava (1762–1839), who might have raised a voice of fierce opposition to Hasidism, were preoccupied with their adamant opposition to and angry denunciation of the menacing secularism of the Haskalah (Enlightenment).

Almost as a general rule, only a fine, not always readily discernible line separates myth from reality in the available varied sources of information concerning the lives of many, especially the early masters of Hasidism. It is therefore the general impression that must often take precedence over detailed accuracy, casting aside the inevitably emerging feeling of uncertainty as to what is real and what is imagined.

Fortunately, more than the accustomed meager ascertainable details are known about Rabbi Eizik (Yitzhak) Taub, the zaddik of Nagykálló (Kálló), the founder of the hasidic movement in Hungary. The Kalever, as he was popularly known, was born in Szerencs (Zemplén county, northeastern Hungary) in 1751. According to tradition, two of his ancestors, Ezekiel (Yechezkel) and Eizik, had fled from Spain in the sixteenth century and after years of tribulation found their way to Hungary and settled in the village of Szerencs. His father, Ezekiel, leased land in Szerencs from Count Almássy and was probably engaged in the cultivation of vineyards and the sale of wine. Ezekiel had two sons, Eizik his firstborn, and a younger son whose name is not mentioned by the sources. Eizik was a weak child, suffering from pain that tormented him throughout his life. His well-to-do father hired a tutor, Rabbi Isaac of Przeworsk (Rzeszow province, southeastern Poland), to whom he entrusted the education of his son. Young Eizik was a bright, receptive pupil; his clear and melodious voice and love of music were his earliest characteristic features. According to custom, he married while still a youth. His first wife—no reference to his second wife is available—was the daughter of Ensil Kaz, a German Jew, and his wife, who was the sister of Eizik's mother. There are conflicting accounts about the subsequent period of his life until be became the rabbi of Nagykálló. According to some sources, young Eizik, dissatisfied with his early marriage, stole away from home and became a pupil of Rabbi Shmelke Horowitz of Nikolsburg (1726–1778), who introduced him to the teachings of Hasidism. After two years of study, however, Rabbi Shmelke found out that his pupil had deserted his young wife and counseled him to return to her. On the way home, Eizik met Yankev Fisch, the respected head of the community of Nagykálló, and became tutor of his children. Some years later he was elected rabbi on Nagykálló. Other sources credit Rabbi Aryeh Leib Sarahs (1730–1791), the famous traveling zaddik, with the discovery of Eizik's unusual intellectual qualities. It was he who allegedly recommended his protégé to Rabbi Shmelke. Eizik was also said to have become the pupil of Rabbi Elimelech of Lyzhansk (1717–1787). Still other sources indicate that Eizik studied for no less than fifteen years in Poland before becoming rabbi of Nagykálló. Whatever the true extent of his studies, Eizik's reported teachers were among the greatest second-generation zaddikim. Although the sheer power and drive of their overwhelming personalities led them to develop different interpretations and applications of the same belief, they had one thing in common that seemed to preserve the semblance of unity: all of them had been disciples of Dov Baer, the *maggid* of Mazhirech (1710–1772), who had succeeded to the leadership of the hasidic movement following the death of its founder, Israel ben Eliezer, the Baal-Shem-Tov (the Besht).

Eminent hasidic masters usually left a lasting impact on their impressionable disciples. Eizik inherited the readiness of Rabbi Aryeh Leib Sarahs to help the needy; he learned the utility of the miraculous stories that surrounded Rabbi Shmelke, and he adopted the practical application of the doctrine of the zaddik that Rabbi Elimelech had advocated.

The County of Szabolcs is situated in the northeastern corner of Hungary. Jews had lived there since the beginning of Hungarian history. It was in Szabolcs, named after one of the thirteen chieftains who led the wandering Magyar (Hungarian) tribes to the conquest of the land that was to become their permanent home in A.D. 890, that the Jewish Khazar soldiers, who had joined the Magyars and fought in their ranks, were settled. They became cultivators of land, breeders of cattle, and traders. For nearly two hundred years they lived there peacefully and unmolested. It was also in that county, however, that the famous Council of Szabolcs was held in 1092 under King László the Saint. It marked the beginning of anti-Jewish legislation which, though frequently disregarded in practice, placed limitations on the rights of the Jews in Hungary. The growing influence of the Church over the Magyars who had become Christians less than a century before and the subsequent vicissitudes of medieval economy, especially in the spheres of trade and commerce, ensured the steady development of animosity of the Hungarians toward the small number of Jews living among them.

Situated in the busy trade route between Transylvania

and Bohemia, Nagykálló had been an important center of commerce since the fifteenth century. Jewish merchants, in quest of opportunity and security, began frequenting Nagykálló in the seventeenth century. By the middle of the eighteenth century, eleven Jews received permission to settle permanently in the city. Jews lived in 83 localities in Szabolcs county. The Jewish community of Nagykálló continued to grow, and by 1752 it numbered nearly 40 individuals. Its steady growth ensured it leadership over other Jewish communities in the county. Joel ben Zvi Bródy (d. 1755), the first rabbi of Nagykálló, was also the first Chief Rabbi of Szabolcs county, a title that his successors held for more than a hundred years.

It was in Nagykálló that Hasidism gained its initial foothold on Hungarian soil. Its initiator was Eizik Taub, who was elected rabbi of Nagykálló and Chief Rabbi of Szabolcs county in 1781. Itinerant hasidic rabbis had often visited Hungary, but none of them stayed long enough to establish a permanent center for the movement. The advent of Rabbi Eizik Taub not only meant permanency for Hasidism in Szabolcs county, but signaled the spread of the movement through the entire northeastern region of Hungary as well. An eloquent and learned representative of Hasidism, his reputation established Nagykálló as the first center of the hasidic movement in Hungary. Yet it was because of the simplicity of his daily conduct that he was to be revered as the first of the Hungarian zaddikim. He was an unpretentious, optimistic, and deeply pious man who belonged to the people, Jews and non-Jews alike, as much as to God. He was frequently found sitting with shepherds at their campfires or in the taverns speaking with fishermen and innkeepers. He listened to their troubles and learned their songs. He was a wanderer, usually accompanied by one or a few of his disciples, who sought out the needy or the sinner and did his best to lessen their suffering or to lead them back into the meaningful religious life of a forgiving community.

The zaddik of Nagykálló earned his enduring fame and

devout following by the purity of his hasidic ideals and conduct. Although himself a pupil of the disciples of the maggid of Mezhirech, the Besht's successor, he usually circumvented his own teachers and established a direct line of relationship to the founder of Hasidism, whom according to legend, he often recalled with love, devotion, and respect, and whose teachings and conduct he sought to emulate. Like the founder of Hasidism, the zaddik of Nagykálló left behind nothing in writing. Only his miraculous deeds and wondrous tales have been preserved in a growing body of oral tradition. Yet his teachings survived recognizably. The centrality of God, which was the very essence of Hasidism, remained the source of inspiration and endurance for him. God was the natural and accessible recourse in times of happiness and trouble. Rabbi Eizik's faith was unshakable. He transmitted it with a smile, in a gentle remark or through the vehicle of a wonderfully entertaining story rather than by thundering exhortation or the threat of heavenly punishment. He eminently fulfilled the fundamental requirements assigned to the zaddikim: he was a trusted and beloved mediator between the two worlds, always ready to bring simple and quick solutions to the needs of the people. His preference for simplicity and the relatively small size of his community spared him from the dangers of externalism, which was to affect the institution of the zaddikim so adversely. He remained an easygoing and straightforward man who felt at home in the company of a few friends and disciples and laid no claim to great fame through riches and the tumultuous crowd of ever-present followers.

The zaddik of Nagykálló enriched the theory and practice of Hasidism with a unique dimension that assured him not only enduring personal fame but the success of the movement in Hungary as well. He was the first hasidic leader who was born in Hungary. He spoke Hungarian perfectly and moved among the non-Jewish Hungarians with ease. According to legend, he utilized many Hungarian folk tunes in religious service and composed a few songs, notably "The

Cock is Crowing Already," which became popular throughout Hungary, and was often seen wearing Hungarian folk costume. He apparently succeeded in breaking through the traditional confines of Jewish exclusivism and was thus largely responsible for the integration of the members of his community into the Hungarian society. His time, to be sure, witnessed the start of the Magyarization of the Jews in Hungary. In that respect, the late eighteenth and early nineteenth centuries constituted a heroic age. With the exception of his ill-fated regulations concerning secular education, Jews responded eagerly to the reforms of Joseph II, which gradually softened the centuries-old, proud, invariably anti-Jewish, exclusivism of independent cities. Progress, however, did not lead to immediate achievement; the Jews of Hungary were to wait more than eighty years before they were legally recognized as citizens of the Hungarian nation. The Magyarization of the Jews of Hungary, however, was by no means a one-sided struggle. Many enlightened non-Jewish intellectuals were responsible for the marked change that was taking place in Hungarian literature. The rigid standards of eclecticism and homegrown prejudice were softened. The accustomed characterization of Jews as being conspiring, malicious, awkward, and ridiculous in comparison with the likable, popular, and ideal figure of the Hungarian peasant gradually gave way to a more enlightened treatment introducing "new" Jewish characters who, by being well-intentioned, industrious, and speaking in faultless Hungarian, became favorably comparable with the traditionally accepted idealization of the national character of the "true" Hungarian.

Rabbi Eizik Taub, the zaddik of Nagykálló, died in 1821 in Nagykálló. In the following year all male Jewish children in Szabolcs county were named after him. For nearly twenty years, the position of rabbi in Nagykálló remained vacant. His grave became a much-frequented place of pilgrimage, especially on the day of *Lag Baomer*.

"Around the lives of the great Zaddikim, the bearers of that irrational something which their mode of life expressed,"

wrote Gershom Scholem, "legends were spun often in their
own lifetime. Triviality and profundity, traditional or borrowed ideas and true originality are indissolubly mixed in
this overwhelming wealth of tales which play an important
part in the social life of the Hasidim." Predictably, the
zaddik of Nagykálló became the subject of a growing number
of stories. By their very nature, the stories might have
removed the real zaddik into the world of wonder and
miracle. But unlike many other zaddikim, whose ascetic,
withdrawn mode of life fired the imaginations of their
disciples and made them the natural object of numerous
legends, with Rabbi Eizik it was the combination of the real
and the miraculous in almost folksy daily conduct and fond-
ness for mysterious stories that aroused the imagination of
his disciples and later admirers. In this first Hungarian-born
hasidic master, strong patriotism and keen awareness of the
society of non-Jewish Hungarians were harmoniously fused
with his uncompromising faith in God and devotion to his
community. He broke through the seemingly inflexible walls
of religious tradition and doctrine when intuition or miraculous signs demanded it. Although his actions often left even
the most faithful of his disciples utterly bewildered, none
of them ever questioned his authority.

The two most easily recognizable traits of Hungarian-
Jewish society have been patriotism and religious identity,
and the authors of the stories about the zaddik of Nagykálló
—Albert Neumann (d. 1943), Lajos Szabolcsi (1889–1943),
and József Patai (1882–1953)—faithfully adhered to that
tradition. It would be difficult to ascertain the origin of the
stories. Some were undoubtedly preserved and transmitted
by the zaddik's disciples; others were probably born in the
imaginations of subsequent generations of pious storytellers.
In retelling the stories about the zaddik of Nagykálló, Neumann, Szabolcsi, and Patai succeeded in combining the
unique elements of the hasidic tale and the characteristic
traits of Hungarian-Jewish life.

RABBI EIZIK

A note on transliteration

Except for minor variations, the system of transliteration of Hebrew and Yiddish phrases and technical terms adopted by the authors of the stories has been followed in order to retain the flavor of the Ashkenazi pronuciation of Hebrew prevalent among the Hungarian Jews and the flavor of idiomatic usage.

1

The Rebbe's Song

Who does not know it! After all people sing it all over the country—that melancholic, sad, yet hopeful song. There is no Jewish wedding or gathering of friends where it is not heard. Amid the merriment, the noise suddenly dies down and intimate conversation turns quiet or stops altogether. Everybody is moved by the song of the "Saint" of Kálló: "The cock is already crowing. . . ." After all, it is his song. The song of the legendary rabbi.

That peculiar song has even been included in radio programs. It is said that one time the *kurucok*[1] sang it. Perhaps. But I know a wonderful story that places the origin of that song in the faraway East in the distant past.

The rebbe[2] of Kálló was an amazing man. He was not a recluse, retiring from the world. He was a great scholar, a noble spirit who looked at the world with eyes of wisdom. His noble heart perceived the divine spark in every living creature. It was only natural that he would be fond of that song. And now that wonderful legend:

It happened at the border of Kálló. The rebbe liked to wander across the fields, especially in early spring, where the sprouting life—like the great hymn of nature—merged with the soul. Suddenly the sound of a flute and the pleasant voice of a boy struck his ears. He stopped. The song was as simple it was beautiful. The Kalever listened with his head bowed. A wondrous sensation of sorrowful remembrance and cherished hope, embedded in the past and soaring into the future, began awakening in his heart. His inner eye could see into the depths of past centuries. In the shadow of the willows of Babylon the same song was played on the harp of the Levites in exile:

> Wait, my rose, wait
> Just you always wait,
> If God willed me for you
> I shall be yours.

The rebbe's enchanted soul soon returned to the present and he found the shepherd boy at the foot of a tree. Drawing nearer he looked at him with his deep, fiery eyes. The boy's hands became limp, his eyes closed, and he fell into a deep sleep. When he awakened, he had forgotten the song.

Toward the close of a Sabbath afternoon, Rabbi Eizik Taub taught his faithful a new song:

The Cock is Crowing Already

> The cock is crowing already
> It will be dawn already,
> In the green forest, in the open field
> A bird is walking.

> But what a bird
> But what a bird,
> Legs yellow and wings blue
> It's waiting for me there.

> Wait, my rose, wait
> Just you always wait,
> If God willed me for you
> I shall be yours.

> But when will it be already?
> But when will it be already?

> *Yiboneh hamikdosh ir Zion temalleh*
> It will be then.

But when will it be already?

The Lambs are Groaning and Moaning

The lambs are groaning and moaning
The shepherds are complaining,
Tell my master
To give hay to the flock of sheep.

But the master replies:
There is the haystack, get it yourself
I haven't seen my herdsman
For a week, or perhaps even three.

There he comes riding an ass,
That's he, as far as I can see.
As long as I am his herdsman
He won't have to worry about the flock of sheep,
As long as I am his herdsman
He won't have to worry about the flock of sheep.

2

The Singing Saint

Once at dinner on Saturday, in the mysterious twilight of the evening when the gates of Heaven are opened and pure souls experience wondrous visions, the zaddik of Lublin[1] turned to his disciples who were sitting around him and said: "In the land of the Hungarians a bright light has become visible, a blindingly glittering star whose brightness originated in the pure days of Creation."

On the following day two of his faithful set out to find that hidden star. They wandered for a long time until they learned that the light for which they had been longing was shining in Nagykálló. They directed their steps toward that small town and reached it on the day before *Pesach*.[2]

As they neared the courtyard of the rabbi, they heard singing and sounds of music. They were amazed, Did *Purim*[3] last until *Pesach* in Nagykálló? As they came closer, the words of the song became recognizable:

> When Israel left Egypt,
> The house of Jacob from strangers . . .

"It must be a *Pesach* psalm," thought the wandering hasids as they stepped into the courtyard.

In the rabbi's house everything was upside down. The zaddik of Kálló prepared *matzoh*[4] at home with the help of his friends. Outside, in the courtyard that was filled with firewood, Reb Chayyim Nachman, the silver-bearded Talmudist, was washing the pots, which had to be changed every five minutes so that the batter stuck to their sides would not rise. In the room, in one of the corners, Reb Chezkel was kneading the batter; his long black beard and hair were covered with white flour. Around the long table, the most distinguished members of the community stood. With their backs bent over, they were pulling and flattening small pieces of batter. Little boys with long earlocks were bustling about carrying the prepared *matzos* to the "sticker," who kept poking a heavy iron stick into the paper-thin leaves so that they would not blister, and from there to the oven, where the rabbi himself sat wearing a white hat. The zaddik was smiling as he stretched a long thin rod toward the approaching children, who skillfully made the *matzos* slide from the kneading boards over it. The burning fire of the oven cast a bright light on the zaddik's glowing face and on his large, white forehead on which there were glittering beads of perspiration.

The sounds made by the banging of the many kneading boards, the scratching of the iron stick, and the pounding of the boys carrying firewood were submerged in the singing of the bakers which, at the zaddik's encouragement, became louder and more spirited. Always the zaddik himself started the songs which, like sparks, flew about from the oven until their light filled the whole kitchen and the courtyard with brightness. In a corner, three Jewish musicians accompanied the singing on fiddle, cimbalom, and flute.

It is said that of all peoples
God worked wonders with us.

And the *matzos* kept stretching to the rhythmical movements of the kneading boards which, in turn, followed the rhythm of the music.

The visiting hasids stood amazed at the doorstep. They had never seen *matzoh* prepared this way.

Reb Chayyim Nachman, who had been scrubbing the pots with feverish speed, noticed the two strangers only after a few minutes had passed. Then he quickly wiped his right hand and stretched it toward the strangers, bidding them welcome.

"*Shalom!* Where are you from?"

"Lublin."

"And where are you going?"

"We'd like to stay with the Rebbe for *Pesach.*"

"When did you leave home?"

The strangers interrupted the questions impatiently. They wanted to see the zaddik for whom they had made that long journey.

"Where is your rabbi now?" they asked.

Old Chayyim Nachman pointed with his thumb at the man who sat in front of the oven, wiping the beads of perspiration from his forehead with his wide sleeves.

Amazed, one of the hasids asked, "But isn't he wearing a 'stranger's' clothes?"

"Those aren't a 'stranger's' clothes, those are Hungarian clothes," replied the old Chayyim Nachmann proudly. "Our rabbi often wears but a shirt at home—a long one reaching the ground and white as snow, of course—because sometimes his weak body cannot bear the weight of clothes. You should see him then! . . . Adam must have been like that in the Garden of Eden before the Fall."

In the meantime, the faithful interrupted their work at the kneading boards for a few minutes, formed a circle around the zaddik, and started dancing to the tune of a psalm.

"Look! How beautifully he is dancing!" remarked one of the strangers.

Reb Chayyim Nachman replied enthusiastically, "You should see how he dances at weddings! He stands in front of the gypsies, has them play a song for him, and dances so that the youngsters gathered there forget about one another and instead of dancing they just stare at the rabbi."

"That's why he does it," interjected another of the zaddik's faithful, whose curiosity had in the meantime led him to approach the strangers.

At that moment, those in the room broke into a new song. But its words were no longer from the Psalms of David, but from one of those sad, melancholic Hungarian songs that the knights, wearing bone-handled muskets and expensive gunpowder pouches, used to sing under the open skies:

> Oh! Beautiful, old
> Magyar people
> The enemy is
> Tearing you to pieces . . .

The two strangers looked at each other in amazement. However, Reb Chayyim Nachmann explained to them that even on the most sacred of holy days the rabbi of Kálló was in the habit of singing Hungarian songs because, he said, the fate of the Hungarians was similar to the fate of the Jews.

When the baking of the *matzoh* was finished, the zaddik rose, wiped the perspiration from his forehead, washed his face and hands, and started to walk out. The faithful followed him.

"The zaddik must be going to the *mikveh*,"[5] said the strangers as they walked slowly after him; "after all, *Pesach* is about to begin."

They were wrong. The zaddik walked on the garden path toward the fields. The trees were already blooming and the rays of the sun broke through the leaves and touched the large field whose green silken carpet was dotted with purple crocuses. Only the singing of birds and the flute of a shepherd boy broke the silence of the sunny spring air. The zaddik stopped in the middle of the field and, gasping, breathed in the fresh spring scent. How beautiful it is to bathe in the air here, how beautiful it is to bathe the soul in songs here. That's the most sacred bathing.

The little shepherd boy slowly started to walk home and, still playing his flute, drew close to the rabbi. The zaddik motioned him closer. "Play that song again for me, my son," he said in a pleading voice.

The little shepherd was moved and repeated the song. The zaddik listened to it with delight. Then he gazed deeply into the boy's eyes and said, "That's a sacred song, my son. It's like the Song of Songs. Play it again."

As if confused by the zaddik's penetrating gaze, the little boy tried but was unable to play the flute. It was as if its voice had become trapped in it. He attempted to start the song a number of times, but to no avail.

"Well, give it to me," said the zaddik, and took the flute from the boy and started playing the song. The soft spring breeze and the rustling of the leaves quieted down, the flowers raised their heads, and the birds, with wide open eyes, cowered on the trees silently listening to the song of the holy man.

The evening fell. With tears in his eyes, the zaddik handed the flute back to the little boy, who was saddened by his inability to play the song, and started walking toward the synagogue.

The zaddik sang the *Pesach* evening prayer to the little shepherd boy's tune. As he sang in front of the pulpit, all of the faithful were quietly humming the song after him. Every soul was filled with the new melody and it looked as if, on all sides, the flickering candlelights were moving their glowing heads to the rhythm of the new song.

When the night fell, the "night of safety" when the harmful demons are in hiding and only Elijah's soul wanders among the houses of the sons of Israel, the house of the zaddik of Kálló looked as if it had been magically transformed. Everything was cleaned bright and shiny for the holiday. On the table, on which hard kneading boards had pounded the thin batter at noon, there was now a white tablecloth and on it many pieces of white dinnerware. In the middle, a large, twelve-branched candelabrum glittered, lighting up the zaddik's face more gently than had the light of the oven at noon. Leaning sideways, the zaddik sat at the head of the table on a sofa with white pillows on it. He wore a festive dress. There were also a few strangers sitting around the table.

The hasids from Lublin waited impatiently to hear some deeply meaningful words of the Torah or kabbalistic secrets from the zaddik's lips. But to no avail. The *Seder*[6] was nearly finished and again they had not heard anything but songs. Psalms in Hebrew alternated with Hungarian songs. The zaddik also sang the *Haggadah*[7] to an unusually gentle tune. Even the story of the ten plagues that afflicted the Egyptians had a deeply sorrowful, commiserating melody.

"Well, we've come in vain," the hasids thought and gave up the idea of waiting for a miracle to happen.

The clock had just struck midnight when the zaddik of Kálló reached the prayer by which the doors in the houses of Israel are opened to welcome the coming spirit of Elijah. The zaddik himself rose and opened the door leading to the street. "Blessed be the one who comes in the name of God."

The zaddik had hardly uttered the words of welcome when suddenly, to the great amazement of the celebrators, the angular figure of an unusual-looking elderly peasant entered the room. He wore a white, shaggy, sheepskin coat and held a shepherd's staff. Stiffly, and with an introspective look in his eyes, he took a few steps forward.

"Blessed be the one who comes in the name of God," repeated the zaddik. He took the visitor by the hand and led him to the table.

The people sitting around the table were terror stricken. They were frightened by the midnight visitor and were afraid that he might touch with his hand that certain cup of wine which had been set aside for the occasion. Silently the old shepherd sat down by the zaddik's side and immediately reached toward the center of the table where stood a large silver chalice filled to the brim with wine.

"The chalice of Elijah! The chalice of Elijah!" the people around the table started shouting, and jumped up from their seats.

The old shepherd quickly drank the wine from the large chalice and then stood up as if going to leave.

"At least, sing a nice song," said the zaddik, who had been looking on calmly. He motioned his faithful to quiet down.

The old shepherd did not reply; he was still preparing to leave. The zaddik continued to coax him in an imploring voice, "Please, do not leave my house without a song."

"Well, so be it," replied the shepherd at last in a voice that resounded as if it had come from another world. "I am going to sing the song that you took from the flutist boy and sanctified." Then he put his right arm around the zaddik's shoulders, "But you must sing with me, too!"

And the zaddik and the shepherd broke into the sorrowful, melancholic song together, "The cock is crowing already. . . ."

The people who sat around the table listened dreamily to the sad song and did not even notice that the mysterious shepherd had suddenly disappeared.

The zaddik kept repeating the song in a sorrowful voice, with insertions in Hebrew about the rebuilding of the Holy of Holies, about Zion, and about the jubilant songs of Redemption:

> The cock is crowing already
> It is dawning already
> *Yiboneh hamikdosh ir Zion temalleh*
> When will it be already?
> *Veshom noshir shir chodosh uvirnono naaleh*
> It is time for it already.

When the two wandering hasids returned to Lublin and spoke of their experiences in Nagykálló with great disappointment, the zaddik of Lublin said the following: "No one has ever come so close to the spirit of the prophet Elijah as the zaddik of Nagykálló. His soul is from the Hall of Songs; all of his sacred deeds become songs. It is with songs that he serves God and approaches Him on the wings of songs so that He will find pleasure in His holy servant."

3

The Miraculous Recovery

A hasid in Galicia was very ill. Not even the best doctors could bring him back to health. In his despair, he went to see his rebbe.

"You are in great trouble, my son," said the rebbe. "There is only one man who can help you. Somewhere in Hungary. Go and look for the Kalever."

The hasid was a well-to-do man and set out on his journey without hestitation. There were no trains then, and travel by carriage was both tiring and complicated.

Even at the border of Hungary, he learned that the Kalever was a great zaddik. People spoke of his wonders. The hasid could hardly wait to see him. Exhausted and deathly ill, he finally arrived. The great rabbi looked at the unfortunate man with a benign smile. "My dear son," he said, "there is an excellent doctor in the neighborhood. His name is Dr. Józsa. Tell him that I sent you. He will try to find out what is ailing you."

The hasid departed. The doctor gave the sick man the friendliest of welcomes and examined him thoroughly. "My dear friend," he said in a sad, resigned voice, "for your trouble I can find no cure."

The hasid returned to the rebbe with a saddened heart. "Do not lose faith, my son," said the rebbe. "Even if medical science fails you, the greatest of all healers, the Lord, may still help you. Return to your native land and you shall have my blessing on the long journey."

The hasid rested for a week and then set out on his journey back. On the third day, in the heat of the sun, he stopped to rest under a shady tree. He was tired and soon fell asleep. In his dream he saw a small, multicolored bird sitting on one of the branches of the tree and singing beautifully. If only he could eat the gizzard of the little bird, he would surely recover.

Suddenly he awakened. He opened his eyes and, lo and behold! the little bird was sitting on a branch within easy reach. He extended his hand, but the bird did not fly away. He caught it and caressed it, then returned to the carriage hurriedly. In the nearest village he had the little bird cooked. In a few hours his pains eased. The journey no longer seemed tiring, and in fact he felt refreshed and as if his body had regained its strength. He was not at all tired when he arrived home.

He told his rebbe of his meeting with the Kalever and of his miraculously fulfilled dream. "I am healthy again," he exulted, "and I can thank a dream for my recovery."

"My dear son," responded the rebbe, "you must also remember the one who sent the dream upon your tired eyes. Remain at home for a few weeks, then return to the Kalever. There you should give praise to the Lord."

He arrived at Kálló earlier than before. The zaddik welcomed him with a smiling face. "May the Healer of all those who are ill be praised!" he exclaimed. "But what about the good doctor? Hurry, my son, let him see you."

The old doctor was working in his garden. He looked up when he heard the gate open. He was amazed at seeing the healthy man and even more so at hearing the story of his miraculous recovery. "What kind of bird was it?" inquired the doctor excitedly.

The hasid recalled the bright feathers and told him everything. The doctor hurried into his house, straight to a large, thick book. He started thumbing it until he found what he was looking for. "Yes, yes," he murmured, "now I know." Then he returned to his guest in the garden. "My dear friend, the bird that you saw in your dream lives only near the Nile River. But it was here now because it was needed. This is not the first miraculous deed of my esteemed neighbor," he concluded, with a mysterious expression on his face.

4

Moshiach ben David and the Prophet Elijah in Kálló

It happened around Purim in Galicia. The great rebbe sat at the table meditating. His hasids looked at his blissful countenance with impassioned eyes. What could he be searching for in the great distance? None of them dared to utter a word or to direct a question to him. Suddenly, they heard a feeble sigh. It came from the rebbe. He began to talk to them quietly in an emotion-filled voice, "If I could spend the Seder at Kálló . . . if I could be there *then.*" He seemed to give the last word special significance. "But it cannot be. I cannot leave my hasids."

The hasids trembled at hearing the mysterious words. A peculiar spell seemed to gain a firm hold over them. Among the hasids there were two rich men who were especially eager to get to the bottom of things. As the others were taking their leave, the two rich hasids approached the rebbe. "We would like to go to Kálló," they said.

"Go, my sons, as soon as you can, so that you may arrive there in time. You will spend the Seder with the Kalever. Keep your eyes open and your hearts in the right place."

The two hasids set out for Kálló. It was an expensive, tiring journey and it was not until weeks had passed that they reached their destination, but they were in Kálló on

37

erev Pesach.[1] The zaddik of Kálló gave them a friendly reception and cordially granted their request to spend the Seder with him. The visitors looked forward to the evening with mixed feelings of expectation and uneasiness. They could hardly wait to sit at the table upon their return from the synagogue.

The rebbe, however, was in no hurry. He paced up and down in his room. He filled his pipe and puffed on it with visible delight. Suddenly he opened one of the cupboards and took a small whip in his hand. He squeezed it hard and swished it forcefully. The hasids looked at each other. Then in a sudden decision, he stepped out into the courtyard. Those sitting in the room could hear the sounds of his steps steps and the swishing of the whip.

"It was hardly worth coming here for this," whispered the two hasids indignantly over the strange Seder. "Did our rebbe send us here for this?"

Soon the zaddik returned, and sat down at the table smiling. He still did not begin the Seder; it was as if he were waiting for something to happen. Suddenly the door opened and a soldier stepped into the room, followed by a woman. They greeted everyone in the room in a resounding voice. The zaddik approached them and said with deep respect, "Blessed be those who enter my house." He paid particular respect to the woman; he kissed her hand. The hasids were thunderstruck.

"My friends," inquired the zaddik, "what brings you here?"

"We came, our master, because we would like to marry," they replied, "and we shall be happy only if you give your blessing to this marriage. We have waited for each other for a long time and after many bitter and tear-filled years, we feel our time has finally come."

The zaddik seemed to be filled with otherwordly happiness. He lifted his hands, and was about to place them upon the heads of the betrothed when he suddenly turned toward his guests. "Will you give your consent to this marriage?" he asked them, almost pleading.

The two hasids were absorbed in their thoughts and were reciting passages from the Psalms as if not hearing or seeing anything. The zaddik slowly lowered his languid arms and an expression of painful disappointment appeared on his countenance. There was silence.

When the two hasids lifted their heads, the zaddik was already sitting at the table. The soldier and the woman were gone. The zaddik started the Seder. Everything went quickly and in a routine manner. They did not see anything unusual, befitting the zaddik's reputation. They were relieved when they could return to their quarters.

The second Seder was no better. The zaddik and his disciples sang an unusual Hungarian song. Although they did not understand the words of the song, their hearts were filled with warmth and affection.

They started their journey home and on the way discussed the events of their stay in Kálló, feeling that they had brought with them no lasting impression. Yet they could not explain that strange rebbe's behavior. The swishing of the whip and the kissing of the hand! What would their rebbe say when he heard the story of the Kálló Seder?

They had hardly arrived when to their great surprise, a message came from the rebbe that he wished to speak with them at once. They hurried to his house and, following a quick exchange of greetings, he urged them almost impatiently to tell him everything. The hasids told him what happened during that strange Seder. There were words of sarcasm and indignation in their description. But what was happening to the rebbe? His countenance became pale and tears were flowing from his eyes. "My children, my poor children," he cried, "you do not know the meaning of your words. The great Kalever is the Almighty's favorite. I only wish my lot were like his. You do not know what you missed. The soldier was Elijah himself and the woman the long-awaited

Messiah. Had you given your blessing to their marriage the
exultant time of salvation would already be here."

The rebbe dropped in his chair and looked at his heart-
stricken hasids with a sadly accusing glance. They started
walking home with their heads bent low. They felt as if a
very heavy weight had been placed upon their souls.

5

He Who Was Caught
in His Own Trap

Do you know who love tales the most? Children! They
would leave their favorite and most entertaining game if you
started to tell them a tale. The zaddik of Kálló was very fond
of children. On Sabbaths he would allow them to gather
around him, and their innocent hearts jumped with joy when
he looked at them with his kind, smiling eyes.

It was going to be a beautiful tale. Purim was approaching,
and it was at that time that the rebbe would customarily tell
his most beautiful tales. The children fastened their faithful,
glistening eyes on the zaddik, whose eyes looked as if they
could penetrate the thick walls of his house.

He began his tale quietly and seriously:

Once, far, far away there lived a mighty king. His realm
was great and his wealth was immense. An army of servants
surrounded him, waiting for his commands. Many strangers
came to his city and among them a Jewish builder arrived
one day. He stopped in front of the king's palace and he
was taken aback by what he saw. "It is amazing," he murmured, "that a king so powerful and wealthy should live in
such an old and unpretentious palace. If he only commissioned me, I would build him such an enchanted palace
that the whole world would marvel at it."

41

At that moment the king leaned out of one of the many windows of his palace and his gaze fell upon the stranger who had been watching his palace. "Bring him to me," he commanded, for he wanted to know why the stranger had been standing there for so long.

The builder came and stood respectfully in front of the king.

"Does your king live in a more magnificent palace?" asked the king upon hearing the builder's explanation.

"Your Majesty," replied the Jew, "do not take offense at my amazement, but this unpretentious palace befits neither your power nor your wealth. I could build you a great and truly majestic palace if you would provide me with the tools and workers I need."

The king agreed. "Let it be."

For many weeks, hundreds of workers, machines, and beasts of burden toiled until the magnificent palace was finished. The king's beaming face revealed his feelings; he could not even dream of anything more beautiful.

"Master," he said, "I want to thank and honor you properly for this masterpiece. Remain in my kingdom."

The Jewish builder became a prominent and respected man. The king respected his knowledge and grew so fond of him that not a day passed without the Jewish builder's coming to the palace twice, where his opinion was asked even on matters of state.

Small wonder that some people began to envy the builder. At first, they whispered only among themselves, but soon malicious rumors reached the king's ears too, but he was so deeply convinced of the honesty of his Jewish favorite that he quickly dismissed them. The enemies of the builder, however, did not rest. One day, when the ruler was in a bad mood, one of his counselors said to him, "My lord, the Jewish builder is not worthy of the many favors you have bestowed upon him. The palace has one great defect. I have recently observed a group of strangers who viewed the palace

snickering. When I asked them the reason for their behavior
they laughed and said, 'Who could build such an ugly palace?
The builder who designed such unattractive windows has
made fun of the king.' Your Majesty, this proves that the
Jew is unworthy of the high position to which you have
raised him."

Gradually the king began to give credence to those who
conspired against his favorite. "Indeed," he thought, "the
windows are ridiculously shapeless. The Jew has made fun
of me. New windows must be installed immediately."

The king entrusted the conspiring counselor to carry out
his orders.

"And what should become of the impudent Jew, Your
Majesty?" inquired the counselor. "For he who arouses the
ruler's wrath is deserving of death."

The king, however, was reluctant to give a quick decision
in the matter. "Tomorrow," he replied. "Tomorrow we shall
decide."

The conspirators were victorious, it seemed.

On the following day, the king sent a sealed letter and
a note of instruction to the Jewish builder. The message
read, "One of my ships has just anchored by the seashore. Go
to it and give this letter to the captain. You will be informed
of the rest there."

"Throw the bearer of this letter overboard," it read. The
captain read the unusual order with surprise. He looked at
the builder with pity. After a moment of hesitation he spoke
quietly to the builder, "I shall not obey the king's order.
It is cruel and unjust. You will put on a cook's uniform and
remain on board in secret. We shall see what the future
brings."

In a few days the ship set out on a worldwide voyage.

The evil counselor rejoiced that the hated rival no longer
stood in his way. Even the king forgot about him. After some
time had passed the ship returned to its home port. When
the king was informed of the arrival of the ship he sent a

message to the captain that he wanted to inspect all the wonderful things the ship had brought from faraway lands.

"Your opportunity is here," said the captain to the builder. "The king will be on board tomorrow. You will put on your old clothes, and when you see the king approaching, jump into the sea from the other side of the ship. I know you are a good swimmer so you will have no difficulty. By the time the king steps on board, you will have swum around the ship and suddenly you will stand in front of him in wet clothes. I shall leave the rest to you."

Thundering music signaled the king's arrival. He stepped aboard, followed by a magnificent entourage. Walking at the king's side, the haughty counselor looked around proudly. Suddenly his countenance grew pale. He turned to the king and whispered with quivering lips, "Look, Your Majesty!"

The astonished king recognized the builder, who now stood dripping wet before him. "How did you come here? What happened to you?"

"Your Majesty," replied the builder, "it is a miraculous story. They cast me into the sea, but I did not perish as you can see. A huge fish swallowed me and took me straight to the King of the Seas. When he learned of my profession he commissioned me to build him a palace. The huge enchanted palace is finished, and only the windows are missing. I did not dare to accept responsibility for them—I have already had bad luck with them. But can anyone imagine a palace without windows? I told the King of the Seas that here in your realm, Your Majesty, there was a famous builder who could make beautiful windows. 'I shall borrow that skillful man from my royal brother on land," said the King of the Seas. 'One of my servants will help you swim to the ship so you may deliver my message.' And now, Your Majesty, the envoy of the King of the Seas is standing before you requesting that you fulfill this wish. The giant fish is waiting at the side of the ship."

Streams of cold sweat poured down the face of the evil

counselor. He could only stammer, as the king's gaze rested on him, "My lord—have mercy on me!"

The king, however, showed no mercy. He turned to the Jewish builder, "My friend, you will stay here, and the counselor will leave to finish my royal brother's palace."

Thereupon the king's men grabbed the trembling counselor and threw him into the sea.

6

Forget-Me-Not

The New Cantor is Coming

In the house of the zaddik of Kálló they knew on the
day of Yom Kippur[1] that something was wrong.

For decades the rebbe used to recite the *musaf*[2] on Yom
Kippur. But on this Yom Kippur the rebbe sat on his chair
motionless, with his head bowed dejectedly, and his hands
slapping his knees. He struggled to raise himself from time to
time but fell back exhausted. His gray locks were disheveled and hanging down his forehead, large teardrops
rolled down his face, and some great pain distorted his features. *"Oy me hoyo lonu,"*[3] he kept whispering, *"Oy me
hoyo lonu."*

The people in the synagogue of Kálló held their breath as
they stared at their rabbi. There was no precedent for this.
When the people finally composed themselves, Reb Dovid
Ettinger, one of the rebbe's confidants, stood by the ark so
that he might recite the *musaf* lest the service be interrupted.
But marvel of marvels! The rebbe would not allow his good
friend to recite the prayer. He interrupted his prayer by
yelling insults at him, so much so that the prayer ended in
confused shouting. On the benches and chairs, the excited
people reacted noisily, and instead of the pure devotion of
Yom Kippur, doubt and anxiety filled the small synagogue.

They went home in the evening, exhausted and trembling, and in the skies, instead of the encouraging sparkle of the stars, menacing, dark clouds gathered. "Great God," they prayed, "what is going to become of us?"

At dinntertime the rebbe gathered some of his disciples around him. Among them was the frightened Reb Dovid whom he had insulted so deeply before all those people. But he embraced Reb Dovid and said sadly, almost moved to tears, "Rebboysem,[4] do not misinterpret what I did today. I did not want you to pray." Every eye turned toward him in astonishment. He continued," I did not want it because I knew that you would be praying in vain. As before every Yom Kippur, I was in Heaven in my vision last night. They usually show me that secret passage, built of emeralds and rubies, through which the prayers recited in all synagogues on earth fly to Heaven. They let me see the doors of the passage leading directly to God's majestic throne. When they are open we may pray joyously for our prayers to pass through the heavenly passages, like fleet-footed wanderers, and reach His presence. But last night, I was shown the passage, and poor me! What I had to see!"

There was hushed silence around the rebbe's table. The people looked at him in awe as tears began to flow down his face.

'Poor me!" the rebbe went on, "the doors of the passage were closed. And in the passage stood the *Yetzer hore*[5] with his armies and the devils laughed when I looked around anxiously. 'Your prayers are in vain, Jews,' they shouted toward me. 'Your prayers will not pass through the passage but into our hands. We shall receive them and break them into pieces like a glass jug. Not one sigh or cry of pain will reach God's throne on this day. We shall get hold of whatever prayer you recite.' "

The rebbe sighed deeply. "And it was for that reason, because I knew what fate was going to befall our prayers on this Yom Kippur, that I did not want anyone to pray in the synagogue. For every word that had left our mouths would have inevitably become the possession of Satan and he would have mockingly thrown our sighs into the mud. Therefore I wanted only abuses and curses to be heard in the synagogue, after all they were to reach only Satan and not our merciful, great God who has turned His love away from us."

"But why, Rebbe? What has happened? How did we sin?" At least ten people asked the frightened questions at the same time.

"I do not really know, but we deserve punishment because the multitude of our sins is always infinite. Rebboysem, I happened to learn that the angels themselves closed the doors of the passage. The angels of the Lord. A terrible accusation was raised against us in front of the throne of God. The enemies of Israel united and brought charges against us. And in order that our prayers might not reach God, the doors of the passage were shut at once. Woe to us! They have already decided to inflict a terrible punishment on Israel. Something horrible is about to happen."

The zaddik of Kálló spoke no more on that evening. Everyone knew what was happening. It became clear to Reb Dovid why the zaddik did not allow him to pray. The people began to fear that great, dark menace that was gathering above Israel.

After that notable Yom Kippur, the rebbe took to his bed. He did not even get up on the Feast of Tabernacles, nor did he even build a *sukkah*[6] for himself. Like a person who has been separated from his friend, he lived barred from God, deprived of heavenly visitors, forsaken and alone, in deep sadness.

Toward Chanukkah, he finally got out of bed. The snow of the month of Kislev[7] was settled on the highway. He watched with melancholy the ornate carriages of the county judges, which passed by on their way to meetings or trials at the county hall. At times a faint spark lit up in his eyes when he looked out toward the white, snow-covered land. "The rebbe is expecting something," whispered the people.

Indeed, the rabbi of Kálló, Reb Eizik Taub, was expecting something. But who could say what? An escape from the great menace, from the invisible horror that was gathering above Israel? A message? But from where?

One day, toward the end of February, a county hussar brought a letter to the zaddik. He was daydreaming in his armchair (he had been doing that for a few days then) and only after the third time he was told of the letter that had been brought for him did he start up in alarm.

"A letter?" the rebbe asked quietly as if talking to himself. "A letter? From the Baal-Shem?"

The people looked at one another. Was the zaddik waiting for a letter from the Baal-Shem? But he had been dead for thirty years. And he could not write to anyone, even to his favorite pupil, the zaddik of Kálló, because the great Baal-Shem no longer used the earthly mail. He was already sitting in his gold armchair up there in Heaven among the pious, the great, and the foremost of Israel. What could the rebbe have been thinking of, expecting a letter from the Baal-Shem?

The rebbe opened the letter sleepily. It was written by the prefect, Count Mihály Sztáray.[8] He informed the zaddik that the new ruler in Vienna, Emperor Joseph, the second by that name, had issued orders for a census involving the population of the counties. His county had already refused once to comply with the order, but the emperor would not give an inch. So the census was taken in the county, also according to religion, and it was found that 1,389 Jews lived in Szabolcs county at that time. And as Emperor Joseph wished to initiate conscription in the county, the count called upon the rabbi of Kálló, the leader of the Jews in the county, to deliver as soon as possible the ten recruits that were the prescribed percentage for 1,389 persons.

The zaddik's face lit up. "Write a letter to the prefect in my name," he said in a stentorian voice, "that we shall deliver twelve, not ten. And those dozen Jews will show how they can fight for the country in the Hungarian style. Send a mounted messenger to Téglás,[9] to Mózsi Oroszlán, the innkeeper, who can deliver six recruits from his family alone."

The faces of the people brightened up at the mention of that name. Mózsi Oroszlán, the Jewish innkeeper of Téglás, and the male members of his family, were the most formidable brawlers in the county. With his father, the old Solomon Oroszlán, he managed the Degenfeld estate and there was no one in the markets who could stand up to them or their children.

After the county hussar penned the answer to Count Sztáray, the rebbe reverted to his daydreaming. He was troubled by that great invisible danger which, like a cloud, was gathering over Israel.

Meanwhile, spring arrived. The ice melted on the Tisza.[10] Tiny violets were blooming in the large meadow at Harangod. The great county carnival had just ended at Kálló, and the counts and their ladies were preparing for the spring socializing. The winds of spring blew throughout the land. It was said that the emperor was losing the war with the Turk and that it would be a good lesson for him and perhaps he would now return their rights to the poor Hungarian people.

The zaddik of Kálló waited and waited. If steps were heard on the porch, he looked out of the window. He watched the passers-by. Judging by the few words he uttered, everyone felt that he was passing through decisive moments. Someone or something had to come with a message.

He often lost consciousness. It was as if he were tensely watching the events of another world, as if he were listening at the gates of Heaven to learn what was happening up there.

On one morning when he awakened, his features showed a great change. His face took on a lively and purposeful expression. Before everything else, he called for the cantor.

"Reb Shmul," he said, "here are two *pengős*.[11] Take your

belongings and move away from here. I've hired a new cantor."

Then he turned—disregarding the laments of the astonished cantor—to his faithful companion, Reb Shayeh Aaron Fisch. "Prepare the horses, Shayeh Aaron and put provisions in the wagon to last for a week. We shall go on a journey."

When the rebbe said something, there was no resisting. The *rebbetsen*[12] prepared the provisions and little Mayerl, the rebbe's son, with his earlocks floating in the air, kept jumping around his father, asking that he be taken along. But no one could sit on the wagon except Reb Shayeh Aaron Fisch and the zaddik. They made room for a third, but it remained empty. In a resounding voice the rebbe called out to his people below, "We are leaving to get the new cantor. *Beshischem.*"[13]

What kind of a new cantor he spoke of, where they had to go for him, and why a new cantor was needed—no one dared to inquire.

The travelers drove away at full speed, along the main street, in front of the county hall, where a liveried attendant stared after the rumbling wagon, and out to the spring meadows, where poppies and daisies were blooming amid the golden sea of wheat. The white farms of Napkor, Apagy, and Ibrony[14] passed by them in the bright sunshine, and the towers of Nyirbátor[15] seemed to be waving to them in the distance. At last they took a brief rest and watered the horses in Demecser.[16] The rebbe lay down in the grass under the open skies and slept soundly until the following morning. Life, strength, and youth returned into his tired and sickly features. They awakened at dawn and pressed on through the steppe of Halász[17] and the farmstead of Bercel.[18] Suddenly, however, something stood in their path as if saying, "You cannot go farther inward. It is my turn now."

The Tisza had overflowed its banks. This was no negligible obstacle. The flood began at Bercel. Small willows disappeared in the waters and the trunks of the red linden trees were covered halfway-up with brown mud that washed away house tops, wash tubs, soldier caps, brooms, branches, and a capsized boat. What a flood! The rays of the sun were dancing on the muddy waves and on the banks, and peasants were shoveling sand desperately by the dyke. The sound of a bell was heard across the river. They gave warning of the approaching flood in Zemplén county. The old bell of Karád[19] was also sounded and the handbells of Gáva,[20] which had not been heard since the days of Rákóczi, answered back, "There is trouble! There is trouble!" And what trouble! The flood kept growing.

His face motionless, the rebbe looked at the despairing Reb Shayeh Aaron Fisch and said, "Well, Aaron, we shall sit down here and wait for the cantor."

If only old Fisch had had the courage, he would certainly have asked, "What cantor? And why do we need a cantor?" But he had not dared to contradict his master for a long time, so he tied up the horses and sat down on a tussock by the rebbe. They threw a tablecloth on the wet grass and listened to the splashing of the water. The Tisza kept growing. They did not speak a word, just looked at the flooded land, waiting.

Well, if the rebbe wanted to wait, he certainly knew that they had to wait. After all, there was a great deal to see as they sat there from morning to noon. What that greedy Tisza carried away! There was a peasant house afloat, perhaps a fisherman's cottage; behind it a doghouse bobbing up and down with its angry dweller inside, and farther on a mail coach was bouncing on the waves. And there, even the rebbe should see this, was a whole island afloat.

A floating island in the Tisza was not a rarity. A flood may tear out a piece of the land and carry it away, from Tokaj[21] as far as Szeged,[22] if it did not change its mind and put it ashore somewhere. The unpredictable Tisza might take a piece of land from one county and hurl it against another.

The island just kept floating down the Tisza. There were a few willows in the front, followed by a fine plot of grass and a small alfalfa field. A small province. And then marvel of marvels! Someone was singing on that floating island.

The rebbe stood up in the midday sun and looked toward the island. Who could be singing there? Who was in such good spirits above the current?

How beautifully that someone was singing on that island! Not in Hungarian, not even in German, but in Hebrew, the holy language:

> *Beni, beni*
> *Al telech bederech ittom*
> *Mena, mena, mena*
> *Raglecho minsivusom . . .*[23]

And with what variations!

First he sang it melancholically with the *shtater*.[24] Then the song began to fluctuate and became sad and emotional as the singer continued with the *woloch*.[25] Finally the *ditke*[26] went up: fast-paced, strong, happy, and humorous. With that, he exhausted all the melodic varieties of hasidic music. And the stranger on the island even clapped his hands to his tunes.

What good humor that man had! It was as if he were traveling in an elegant carriage, sitting on a silk pillow, instead of fluttering on a small piece of land above the raging current.

His arms stretched wide, the rebbe stood on the shore. His figure was as majestic as that of a Moses standing amid the waves of the great Egyptian sea. Lo and behold! The next current jarred the island out of course and started to push it toward the shore of Bercel, where the zaddik of Kálló waited.

The island kept floating closer and closer. The figure of the stranger became visible. He was a huge man with a black beard. He sat under a willow. His kaftan fluttered in the fresh breeze. His eyes glittered. And he sang and sang.

Reb Shayeh Aaron Fisch stiffened in his amazement. He just kept staring at the unusual vision, unable to utter a word. The island arrived; it hit a tussock and bogged down. The new cantor touched land in Szabolcs county. The rebbe waved his hand. "*Sholem aleychem!*" he shouted toward the stranger.

It must be admitted that that was an unusual spectacle at the Bercel shore: An island floating down the Tisza; on the island a lost stranger, his name, origin, purpose, unknown. Yet, when the island touched land, a huge, gray-haired man welcomed him on the shore as if he had been waiting for him. He embraced him as if he knew him. He brushed the thistles off his clothes as if he were his own son who had arrived suddenly.

It was no less conspicuous that the stranger, whom the Tisza brought to Szabolcs and into the arms of the zaddik of Kálló, was not surprised in the least—as if it were only natural that he would be welcomed in such manner. He even smiled when he looked back at the floating island, which dangled in the whirling water like an obedient ferry.

"I've had quite a good journey, thank God," he said. "For a day and a half I traveled as comfortably as a *purets.*"[27]

"Do you know that we've been waiting for you?" asked the zaddik. As for himself, Reb Shayeh Aaron Fisch was so astonished that he could not even ask questions. The stranger kept smiling.

"I have a letter in my pocket," he said, "addressed to Reb Eizik Taub, the rabbi of Kálló. As the Lord directs mortals on their paths, I've been wandering the four corners of the earth for half a year so that I may deliver this letter to whom it is addressed. And if I was not carried away by the Tisza, if the peasants of Zemplén[28] did not beat me to death, and if the water put me ashore so gently, then only God, may His name be blessed, knows my destination. He sent me to the place where I must take this letter."

That was too much for Reb Shayeh Aaron Fisch to bear.

"But who are you, anyway?" he blurted out excitedly. "How did you get here? And how come you know who we are?"

"Enough of the questions, Shayeh Aaron," the rabbi of Kálló tried to calm his faithful servant. "Why ask all those questions when I already know the answers. And this Jew here knows well, too, that I am the Kalever, the rabbi of Kálló. The Baal-Shem sent that letter, the Baal-Shem, my illustrious master, may his memory be blessed among the tens of thousands of Israel. We need a cantor in Kálló because the old *chazzen*[29] left. So, we sat down by the bank of the Tisza and waited for a cantor. And the cantor has come! The water brought him and we could hear even above the sound of the waters a voice praising God. It was the voice of this Jew. He sings well, so we shall hire him. We shall take him to Kálló. And that is all, Shayeh Aaron. Fetch the horses and let's go."

Shayeh Aaron gasped like a fish out of water. He had never been given an explanation for a miracle in such a way, that was certain. What could he do? He started harnessing the horses and left the stranger alone with the zaddik.

As soon as they were alone, the zaddik changed completely. His face turned red; he embraced the stranger excitedly and trembling, and asked in a barely audible, emotional voice. "Where do you come from and what is your name, my son?"

"I come from the mountains, Rebbe," responded the stranger, his head bowed down. "From the mountains? No. even farther. I come from great sadness, destruction, and forlornness. A curse is following me, Rebbe, and Satan, too. I come from afar, beyond the borders and I am looking for a place where I may rest. My name is Chayyim Weinstein and I used to be an innkeeper in a village at the bottom of the Carpathians in Galicia."

The zaddik of Kálló put a finger to his lips, "Enough, Reb Chayyim, not a word more. I don't want anyone to hear of our secret. Let's get on the wagon. Listen to me, we are going back to Kálló. When Shayeh Aaron, my faithful companion, becomes sleepy I shall take the reins out of his hands. Until then you'll sleep inside the wagon. I shall awaken you in the evening and you will sit up there, next to me. We shall ride at an easy pace. And then you will tell me everything and I shall listen to you. Throughout the whole night."

"Wherever I go," the stranger sighed, "clouds gather above the Jews. It isn't safe to take me in because Satan is after me." The zaddik nodded, "I have known about it, felt it, and waited for it since Yom Kippur. What about the letter, Reb Chayyim?"

"It is in the pocket of my kaftan. It's been waiting for thirty years to be opened."

They got on the wagon. Shayeh Aaron Fisch sat proudly in the driver's seat and behind him, hidden in his shadow, the zaddik crouched. The stranger stretched himself out inside the wagon, under the canvas, and soon fell asleep.

Forward, Thunder! Step lively, Hussar! It was necessary to use the whip from time to time because the horses were unpredictable. One was slow; the other kicked up his hind legs occasionally. Anyhow, it was not easy to drive such an overloaded wagon in the sandy steppes of Szabolcs. They could not take the road back on which they had come because it was blocked by the gendarmes and the laborers of the county who were working fast to build a dyke against the great flood. One cart came after another. The zaddik and his companions had to take another road leading southward toward Dombrád[30] and Tass.[31] There were also nobles driving their carriages on the road—large carriages, each drawn by eight horses. The Kállays, the Osváths, the Leöveys, and the Dessewffys[32] were riding at full speed to watch the flood.

That unpretentious Jewish wagon, the wagon of the zaddik of Kálló was forced to stop at the side of the road, often for long hours. Reb Chayeh Aaron, aside from the heavy perspiration he worked up in goading the horses, began to experience some unusual things. Here and there, piercing looks and angry eyes stared at the wagon. Peasants coming from the opposite direction shook their fists and shouted, "Damned Jew, where are you running from the water?"

It was unusual to hear that kind of talk in the area. But things became more serious when the rough talk stopped. A stone was thrown into the wagon, almost hitting the zaddik of Kálló on the head. It was accompanied by a shout, "No Jew should drive a wagon, dammit!"

Well, well. How those fine, patient, and honest people of Szabolcs have changed! as if they had become a completely different people. They were throwing stones at the zaddik's wagon, yet the day before they had even tipped their hats to him. Perhaps the flood caused all that excitement among them.

The zaddik of Kálló nodded and quietly said, "Don't be frightened, Shayeh Aaron. It had to happen."

The setting of the sun reached them near Berkes, at the rest place of *kuruc* soldiers. The sky was covered with dark heavy clouds, the sounds of the flood were heard in the distance, also the growing, sad rumble of tolling bells. Bad times had come to Szabolcs county.

The zaddik told Shayeh Aaron to let the horses rest and feed them because he expected to travel all night long. Then he told him to awaken the cantor and get some sleep himself. The zaddik himself was going to drive the horses that night.

Indeed, the zaddik had taken the reins into his own hands. Reb Shayeh was already asleep on a pile of hay inside the wagon, and the cantor was still rubbing his eyes as he looked around the peaceful countryside. It was already evening, and the crickets were chirping in the fresh, dew-covered grass. Above the small puddles, dragonflies were buzzing. The new crops released their sweet smell; the large green and golden tracts of land gradually faded into the darkness. Those were small stars rising up there, the little lanterns of the Nyirség,[33] by which God showed His pious people the way home.

The hooves of the horses clattered on the road. The zaddik lit his pipe and blew large rings of smoke into the swarms of mosquitos. The cantor also stuffed his pipe.

It was quite dark by then.

"And now speak, Reb Chayyim . . ."

There was a short pause. The dark figure of a peasant passed by the wagon. Then the stranger started speaking in a quiet, melodic voice.

"I was an innkeeper for thirty years in the village of Smihov, up in Galicia. I was not yet eighteen when I and my Hendeleh moved to the mountains, where I leased a tavern from my father-in-law, who was a rich man. We lived happily there, on the slopes of the Carpathians where the air is so clear and the sky and God are so near. We had everything; the babbling of children and the happy sounds of talmudic studies in the morning and in the evening filled the house. The peasants liked us, and we could even put aside a little money in the drawer. The tavern was full; wandering Hungarians, traveling Germans, and many soldiers took their rest there. We even had to enlarge the shed because it was no longer big enough for the many carts and for the relay horses of the mail. Amid these days of happiness and prosperity, a large group arrived by carriage at noon. A huge, gray-haired rabbi was the leader. He was accompanied by many other rabbis and two young men. I learned that the old man was the great Baal-Shem, who was on his way to Berlin to visit a very sick person. He looked around in my nice, clean room in which everything sparkled, and noticed my books, the volumes of the Talmud, the picture of my parents, and the *Yahrzeit*[34] tablets. He could feel with his great heart that he was staying with happy and contented people. While my wife was preparing dinner for his people, he quietly asked me if I needed anything. I replied, 'All that I need is to remain strong and healthy and besides that I wish for nothing else.' The Baal-Shem looked at me with his big, black eyes and asked for a pen and paper in an unusual, regretful voice. 'I am going to write a letter to someone in Hungary. Deliver it, Reb Chayyim, should your travels ever take you there.'

"He sat down by the table and wrote the letter. I put it in the pocket of my mackinaw and promised him that in the coming week, when I was going to travel to Ujhely to purchase wine, I would deliver the letter. I did not even bother to see to whom it was addressed. Then the Ball-Shem ate dinner with us and when, during the aftermeal prayer, he reached the line *Horachamon hu yisbayr oleynu meal tzavoreynu,*[35] his eyes were filled with tears. I went out to the stable to harness the horses and as I placed the bridle on one of them I bent over and the letter fell out of my pocket into the toolbox. I did not even notice it in the great excitement. When he got on the carriage, the Baal-Shem once more called out to me below,'*Di zolst mir immer bitochn hobn im Aybershten, nor bitochn, immer bitochn.'*[36] Then they disappeared in the mountain roads. The letter remained in the toolbox in the stable. I forgot about it completely."

He sank into silence because some drunken youths were approaching on the road. They stopped suspiciously when they noticed the dark wagon in the night. One of them lifted his lantern, which threw its light into Reb Chayyim's worried face. Immediately, the satirical song rang out:

I have been a Jew, too.
For all that.
I stretched leather in the cold,
And my back ached, too.
For all that.

Jew, Jew, shabby Jew!
Have you got a rouge?
If you sell it, buy it back,
And smear it on your beard.

The loud singing roused the farm dogs from their sleep. They started howling. The zaddik cracked his whip to speed up the horses and said quietly, "I have never heard such songs around here."

When they reached a quieter area, he turned again to the stranger, "And what have you done since then, Reb Chayyim?"

"What have I done? I built. I built a house for myself. Not down here, however. I had learned from my forefathers that if a man lives honestly and piously then he is slowly building a house. Up there, in Heaven. Every good deed, every prayer, and every night spent in study means as many bricks on that heavenly building, on that *binyan shel maaloh*. My house up there was almost finished because I led a pious and God-fearing life on earth. But then Satan noticed my house and felt that he had to lead me into sin. If I stopped living piously and sinned, that house up there would collapse and there would be one less pious man around the throne of the Lord. Satan tried to tempt me."

The two men huddled closer to each other. "Yes, he tried to tempt me, Rebbe. He took away my wife and my children died. They carried five little coffins out of my courtyard. My house burned down. Trouble and misfortune befell me day after day. Perhaps all that happened so I would abandon my trust and faith in the Lord, even for a moment; so that I would reject His providence and rebel against Him. But Satan could not deter me. I remained strong. My heart was bleeding, but I kept praying. My soul was broken, but I remained faithful.

"My business was ruined, and gradually I sold everything. I remained alone, like a dried-out tree whose branches were broken off. About half a year ago I looked around in my house searching for anything I could sell. I found some leather straps in the toolbox. As I was pulling them out of it, a yellow, smudgy envelope fell to the ground. It was the letter, the Baal-Shem's letter that he gave me thirty years before and that I forgot to deliver.

"And then I started out with the letter. I left my dilapidated house, which had once been my happy home, around Yom Kippur and came to Hungary. Trouble and curse followed me, however. Satan would not leave me. Cholera broke out in the village in Sáros county where I slept the first night. They chased me out with pitchforks. In Zemplén, the peasants pursued me, thinking that a witch dwelled inside me. They chased me as far as the shore of the Tisza, where I hid in the mangrove. They would certainly have found me had it not moved away from the shore and had the Tisza not carried away that small piece of land. They stood there staring as I floated by before their eyes. And on the waters of the Tisza I began to feel God's helping hand again and I did not stray away from Him. The praising of God blossomed in me, like a rose on the rock, and I knew then that Satan would never tempt me again. And I began singing of God and the rebbe was already waiting for me on the shore."

The dawn was breaking in the east. They had covered a good deal of land during the night, nearly a half of the county. Then the silver-peaked tower of Kiskálló became visible. The rebbe was silent for a long time. Then he turned to the stranger. "Give me the Baal-Shem's letter."

He opened the letter in the small light of dawn. The large, solemn letters of the Baal-Shem lit up on the yellow sheet, "I, Rabbi Israel of Myedziborz, am sending you, my son and favorite pupil, this writing. I am giving you and all of Israel notice of trouble and misfortune. Help the man who brought you this letter for he has been tested by God as He shall test you, too. Be strong and have faith in the Lord who selected you for suffering and forbearance, for teaching and exemplification. I, Rabbi Israel, have written you this."

Tears gathered in the eyes of the zaddik of Kálló. Then he composed himself and looked up. "Do not fear, my son. We shall go together toward the *yisurim*,[37] and victory and happiness will be ours. And if we stand the test well, God will find pleasure in us."

Reb Chayyim trembled. "I feel, Rebbe, that fate is after

us. Satan is following us. Perhaps in the form of that white
dog trotting after us. Perhaps in that patch of cloud flying
above us. Perhaps in the shadow our wagon casts on the
ground."

A weathered tavern came into view on the highway. The
zaddik of Kálló stopped the horses. "Reb Shayeh Aaron,"
he shouted into the wagon, "we are at the Forget-Me-Not.
Get up and let's pray the *shacharis*."[33]

Indeed, there in front of them stood the Forget-Me-Not,
the famous tavern at the border of Nagykálló, to which
the gentlemen of the county so often came to have a good
time. The Forget-Me-Not, with its shaky beams, its gray-
haired, surly innkeeper, and his beautiful daughter.

Lively tinkling of glasses was heard through the doors.
There was still great merriment in the Forget-Me-Not.

It Would Have Been Better To Stay at Home

Three gypies were playing at the long table of the
Forget-Me-Not. Sitting at it was Mózsi Oroszlán, the first
Jewish soldier in the county, having great fun. His hat was
cocked over his eyes and his blue dolman, on whose lapel
large, red wine spots were visible, was unbuttoned. He
attempted to sing a song in the raspy voice of a drunkard
while pushing a large jug in front of him back and forth.
Occasionally that good wine of Homok splashed out of the
jug. Then he grabbed his sword, struck the table with it
and broke into sighs, "Forget-Me-Not, Forget-Me-Not. . . ."

Looking somewhat pale by the morning light, the object
of his affection stood by the table. Her hair fell on her
shoulders as was the custom of city ladies, rather than tied
in a pigtail like the hair of peasant women. She looked at
the sighing soldier with her blue eyes, and at the gypsies who
kept winking at her. She was the innkeeper's beautiful
daughter, Forget-Me-Not, whose real name was Rozália

Cserepes but whom the whole county and the people of the highway simply called Forget-Me-Not. She was indeed like the forget-me-nots in the fields: simple, gentle, sweet, and a little flirtatious, too. She was very proud of the fact that no man had ever kissed her, although the subprefect and the county clerk often stopped by at the tavern, and there was even a jurist in the county hall who put the beauty of Forget-Me-Not into verse. Yet the forever-smiling, rcd, cherrylike lips remained unkissed. It was her ornament and pride, and she often said that if someone were to kiss her she would leave home. The silly thinking of a girl! Who was to blame for that?

Mózsi Oroszlán was in love with Forget-Me-Not. It had already started back home in Téglás where he, too, had a tavern. He used to steal away from his father, old Solomon, often for days, in order to court the daughter of the innkeeper of the Forget-Me-Not. Since he became a soldier, after the zaddik of Kálló had had him and eleven of his companions recruited to fulfill the quota prescribed for the Jews of Szabolcs, he was stationed at Kálló, from where he went out to the border of the county every day. He became the most faithful guest at the Forget-Me-Not Tavern. There he would start sighing in front of the blue-eyed angel, as it happened on that morning, too. "Forget-Me-Not, Forget-Me-Not . . . Give me a kiss and God will bless you for it."

But Forget-Me-Not just laughed. She was used to hearing that plea. But she replied quietly, revealing the secret of her heart, "I can't do it, Mózsi. You know that I am bound by my pledge."

"I know, I know," moaned Mózsi. "Hey! It's that fellow on the Turkish border!"

That young man on the Turkish border had the key to the red lips of Forget-Me-Not. He was from Kálló, an upright craftsmen and the fiancé of the innkeeper's beautiful daughter. When Emperor Joseph went to war with the Turk, he took him away to serve as a gunsmith. The young man had been gone, stationed along the Száva River, for nearly a year, but Forget-Me-Not remained faithful and did not break her bridal oath even once.

Mózsi Oroszlán was daydreaming. It occurred to him that it was not right that what Forget-Me-Not allowed one soldier of the emperor she denied another. It was quiet in the tavern. The quiet of the early morning. The gypsies lowered their fiddles; one or two sat with their heads lowered. However, inside Mózsi Oroszlán, the wine began to boil. He got up from the table and staggered toward the girl.

"Forget-Me-Not," he stammered, "listen to me. I am going to the battlefield, too. I love you, too; and I deserve a kiss from you, too."

The staggering man frightened Forget-Me-Not. She moved to the opposite side of the table. Mózsi Oroszlán's eyes were throwing sparkes. He flexed his formidable muscles and his face turned red. He leaned on the table with his arms, with which he had broken a pine tree in half the week before.

"Why, if you don't give one," he yelled, "I am going to take it for myself! I'm not going to chase around the table."

And marvel of marvels!—he lifted that table made of oak, at which a dozen people usually sat, and threw the huge, heavy structure into the wine cellar. Its crossbars broke like reed sticks under the terrible weight of the table. The gypsies jumped up frightened and ran out of the tavern. There were no more obstacles to the kisses of Forget-Me-Not. Mózsi stood there with his shirtsleeves rolled up on his arms and only a faint, astonished scream left the girl's lips. In the next moment, the soldier grabbed and kissed her.

Like a wild cat, Forget-Me-Not tore herself out of the arms of Mózsi Oroszlán. Her face was bleeding from scratches, tears filled her blue eyes, and her mouth twisted because of the great injustice just done to her. She had been kissed! She ran to the door and from there she screamed back at the staggering soldier, "Nobody is going to see me ever!"

And with that she ran out to the highway. It was at the same moment that the wagon of the zaddik of Kálló stopped in front of the tavern. Reb Eizik was getting down from it, exhausted by the unusual night. Reb Shayeh Aaron was attending the horses. The third, the stranger, was about to enter the tavern when Forget-Me-Not ran into them like a wind storm. The shame of the kiss was burning on her cheeks. She nearly knocked them down. She ran past them out into the fields. Her white figure became smaller and smaller and soon she was no more than a faint dot among the green crops. And then the dot disappeared, too. Forget-Me-Not ran away.

An unusual silence settled on the fields. Nobody had yet awakened. The shepherds were asleep, and so were their flocks and komondors.[39]

The zaddik of Kálló looked at these happenings with amazement, and stood bewildered in front of the tavern for a long time. Then staggering and with arms dangling, Mózsi Oroszlán appeared in the doorway. He tried to hum a rowdy song, but the cool morning air that touched his forehead suddenly sobered him up. He gave an uncertain look at the three Jews standing by the wagon. Then he recognized the zaddik of Kálló. He bowed and kissed his hand. The zaddik said in a serious and harsh voice, *"Moishe, di bist scho wider shiker!"*[40]

Mózsi Oroszlán stood perplexed in front of the zaddik. Then, as much as his heavy tongue allowed, he started explaining. An hour passed and the innkeeper of the Forget-Me-Not suddenly appeared at the door. He was looking for his daughter, "Forget-Me-Not, my daughter! Where are you?"

The tavern was empty. There was no sign of Forget-Me-Not. Her father looked around puzzled, then frowned when he noticed the three Jews on the highway. Bálint Cserepes, the owner of the Forget-Me-Not Tavern, was not fond of Jews. Then he called out again for his daughter. But Forget-Me-Not was nowhere. The stammering of Mózsi Oroszlán outraged him even more. The veins swelled on his forehead.

"Jews!" he yelled. "What did you do with my daughter?"

Then he started to run on the highway toward the neighboring houses and farms screaming, "People, good people, help! The Jews killed my daughter!"

Two hours later they marched into Kálló—the zaddik, his two companions, and the soldier. All of them were in chains. The Jews of Kálló watched their leader in dismay as he walked surrounded by gendarmes on the main street, with his head raised high amid the vulgar shouts of the mob. They were headed straight toward the county jail.

A great deal of time, two hours. In two hours the sunflower may droop if it does not see the sun; in two hours a new bud can blossom on a branch after the rain; in two hours the bold dayfly comes into existence and withers away. And in two hours the rumor of a ritual murder accusation at the Forget-Me-Not Tavern spread among the farms.

It was not a newcomer in Szabolcs; the bloodthirsty stranger had been there already and was about to come again. It had been hiding in the marshes or deep in the forests. It slept in the darkness of barns and lurked in the dimness of sheds. And when it felt that its time had come, when the air was thick and the souls were filled with sorrow, it started to crawl forth. Walking slowly, like a highway robber, like a firebug, it set fire to the smallest houses; then the flames penetrated deeper and deeper. Suddenly, souls were afire and hands clenched into fists. Amid the flames, wearing a red cloak, with its satanic face it appeared: the Accusation, the eternal, the horrible Accusation.

Forget-Me-Not had disappeared. There were blood stains —could they not have been the stains of wine?—on the floor.

A Jewish soldier in the tavern; three Jewish strangers in front of it. One of them had never been seen in the area, someone whom the zaddik of Kálló brought here for *that* purpose. After all, the zaddik of Kálló himself was there. The leader of the Jews in the county. A zaddik. And then the witnesses came: the gypsies, who saw Forget-Me-Not struggling with Mózsi; the shepherds, who saw her flee with blood on her face; and someone else who saw nothing, only heard something. A scream. It was all too clear; they finished off the girl on the field and they must have buried her there, too. They will find her body. And that Mózsi was lying that he only wanted to kiss her!

For the time being, into the jail with the scoundrels! Let the pandours of the county, the gendarmes, and the neighboring scythemen come forward! Let those Jews be bound!

The stranger sobbed when they bound him; Reb Shayeh Aaron kept shaking his head. A quiet smile seemed to appear on the zaddik's face. However, a dozen men were needed to tie up Mózsi Oroszlán, because he had already struck six men on the head so violently that they fell down by him in a faint.

They were all bound, and that was the main thing. The gendarmes escorted them into the jail. The mob threw rocks at them and Count Sztáray, the prefect, looked out of the window of the county hall with an indifferent smile on his face. Then the mob turned on the houses of the Jews. Looting, ravaging, and screaming filled the Jews' street. Orders were issued for the arrest of wealthy Jews. The suppressed soul of the people, embittered by the flood, the bad harvest, and the emperor, gave free course to its wrath against the Jews. A blow at the Jew was also a blow at the emperor who was such a good friend of the Jews.

The four prisoners marched across the courtyard of the county hall in the great commotion. The warden already had the doors of the jail unlocked.

The cantor started lamenting, "I brought this terrible thing upon you. All this is the work of Satan, who has been after me. I am the guilty one, Rebbe."

Reb Shayeh Aaron just shrugged his shoulders and blurted out the following wise statement: "It would have been better to stay at home . . ."

Mózsi Oroszlán shook the heavy chains on his wrists.

"If Samson brought down the palace of the Philistines," he grumbled, "I can surely break these few bricks. I am going to break this jail open and rip up the gates. We aren't going to stay here for long!"

Only the zaddik of Kálló kept walking calmly amid all the excitement. And with a quiet smile on his lips he uttered the following memorable words, "God is angry with us, my sons. He is angry with us, with Israel, as He has been so often. He is angry with us, as is the husband with his sinful wife. Our sins have angered, outraged Him. And at the time of His anger, He has sent us, as the husband to his wife, a *sefer kerisus*.[41] But we shall not accept it, my sons. In ancient times, He sent it with the prophets in the form of their exhortations. We did not accept it because we did not want to be separated from Him. He sent it with executioners in the days of the Spanish Inquisition. Each stake was a letter of divorce because the angry Creator wanted to be separated from His people. But we did not accept it then either. And now He is sending us a letter of divorce to show that He will withdraw His helping hand from us, that He will forsake us, that He will let us suffer, and that we are no longer His people. My dear sons! We shall not accept it at this time either. We shall remain faithful to Him, we shall return to Him, we shall place our trust in Him, and we shall never forsake Him. We are His and He is ours in light and in dark, in freedom and in servitude!"

The iron gate of the county jail closed with a loud bang behind the four Jews.

The Kálló Double

The story was simple, indeed.

A girl disappeared from a tavern at the border of Kálló on a fine, spring morning. At the same time, three Jews were found in front of the tavern, and the fourth was a drunken soldier, who had been hanging around the girl for a long time. Love? Not in the least. He wanted her blood. The three Jews plotted the murder and the fourth carried it out. Then they buried the girl somewhere in the fields. Was there anything more simple in the world?

It did not matter that the Jews denied it. It did not matter at all. The four jailed Jews kept denying it—the zaddik, Shayeh Aaron Fisch, Chayyim Weinstein, the stranger, and Mózsi Oroszlán. They kept asserting that the girl, that certain Forget-Me-Not, ran out into the fields and that they should search for her there and would surely find her.

They had been in jail for three weeks and still arrests were made day after day. Yosef Mandel, the rich leaseholder of Kálló, was arrested. So were Reb Yosef Nánás and his brother, Mechl Nánás (they had no real family name but the name of the town from which they came), Reb Modche Tarcal, and the old Reb Aaron Patak, the most devout Jew in the community. And who could remember how many more? Some thirty Jews sat in the musty jail of the castle of Kálló.

The fine spring days passed. Here and there a Jewish house was set afire; robberies and brawls broke the quiet of the Jews' street. Investigating on their own initiative, a few enterprising Jews searched the area. They were looking for Forget-Me-Not. But nobody knew anything about her. Nobody in the village or on the farms. The ferryman on the Tisza did not see her, nor did the wandering shepherds. That girl disappeared; the earth swallowed her, the Tisza drank her. Nothing remained of her but her name.

A month later the county court began its preparations. The county judges arrived in their covered carriages; even some eminent jurists came from the cities. István Eördögh, Esq., a lawyer from Debrecen,[42] was to represent the innkeeper's case. The news went around that Count Sztáray, the prefect—or if he did not, his deputy the heavy-handed Kállay—would sit in the first row in the county courthouse.

It was also said on one day that gallows were erected at the edge of the town.

As far as the Jews were concerned, there was only one big question that excited them: What was the zaddik of Kálló doing? What was their zaddik doing in his great loneliness on the dark floor of the jail?

It was a narrow cell, hardly six feet in length, with bars in its window. There was an unplaned table and a stone bench in it. Reb Eizik Taub, the zaddik of Kálló, had been its occupant for a month.

He was not unhappy in that terrible cell. There was almost always a smile on his pale lips. He spent half of the day praying, the other half studying. They allowed only a few books to be brought into his room. The *Shaare Zion,* the holy prayer book of Luria and Vital, which always lay open in front of him, and a small, hand written book, the *Sefer Nitzochon,* the *Book of Victory.* It was those books that he kept reading, and he remained in good spirits.

He answered the judges quietly; he spoke the truth, simply, wisely, and firmly. Of the "murder" he knew nothing.

He was not permitted to receive visitors. Once in a while a shadow passed by outside the bars, but he paid no attention. He studied, prayed, and meditated.

In the midde of the night, when the steps of the guard would fade away in the corridor, the mysterious light of a wandering lantern would break the loneliness of the zaddik of Kálló. The big lock opened, the bolts crackled, and someone entered the cell and sat down on the stone bench next to the rabbi, who was keeping awake in the dark. When the visitor placed the lantern in front of him, its light revealed his handsome face, his white French wig, and his carefully assembled attire. He was a tall, fine-looking young man. His name was Szentmarjay, the secretary of the prefect of Szabolcs county.

He was a revolutionary. Anger and hatred incited his soul against the rule of the county and the nobles. He wanted to create a new, better, and finer nation in place of the old. A nation of Hungarians without nobles and county judges, without serfs and servants. Like a sensitive timepiece, his soul was turned toward Paris, where the earth shook and the ancient regime faltered at that time. In the daytime he performed his duties with tight lips; in the afternoon he was engaged in secret correspondence of a varied nature with a few friends in hiding, with a certain Ignác Martinovics[43] and Ferenc Kazinczy[44]—and with Paris. And whereas in the daytime he had to keep in order those shameful files of the ritual murder case of Kálló; at night his excited and troubled heart took him to the Jews, to the rabbi's cell. He was drawn to those persecuted people since he was persecuted himself. He sensed some great, ancient wisdom and knowledge in the rabbi with whom he sought refuge at night. The Jews and the new era, he felt with brooding anticipation, belonged together.

Each night Szentmarjay inspected the jail. The prefect, he said, wanted to know even the dreams of the guilty Jews. But the truth was that, instead of inspecting the jail, he sat down in the zaddik's cell after midnight and kept awake with him until dawn.

It was an unusual midnight scene by the flickering light of the oil lamp. Side by side on a stone bench a fashionably dressed, stately young man and the old rabbi.

"They are weaving this terrible, monstrous accusation around you," Szentmarjay whispered often, "and they believe it religiously. They even have witnesses to it. That old foolish superstition . . . Often I clench my fists and must restrain myself from pouncing on them. At the tea parties of the prefect's wife, they talk about nothing else but the four gallows. That's how they spend their time. That's their problem. And the world is already aflame in western Europe. The national assembly is meeting in Paris . . . liberty and fraternity!"

The zaddik just smiled mysteriously.

"Where do you get your peace of mind, Rabbi?" gasped the young man. "Aren't you afraid? Aren't you trembling? You are forsaken in this desert. You are alone. They are after you."

At such times the zaddik would answer quietly, "Our religion says 'Be among the persecuted rather than among the persecutors.' I am waiting for God!"

A week later, Ferenc Szentmarjay stepped into the rabbi's cell in great excitement.

"I cannot bear it any longer," he whispered, "I cannot bear it. I sent a letter to the Emperor through secret channels. He is in Lugos on his way back from the war. He is fond of you. Joseph is a friend of the Jews. I wrote him what the county, his chief enemy, is about to do with you: burn Jews, like in the Middle Ages and conduct a witchcraft trial for the shame of the monarchy. I asked him to order the release of the Jews and an official search for the girl. They will find that girl! Oh! If only Joseph would come! He is a revolutionary, a free thinker, like us, the youth. If only he would come with his soldiers to destroy that old county hall, that owl-haunted place, that nest for bats . . . Give us light, otherwise we'll go blind! You Jews are fond of light, aren't you? If only you would unite; we could carry out a revolution with you easier than with the peasants. We'd unite you who are without rights, shabby, and persecuted, if only you listened to us and marched with us."

The zaddik of Kálló cast a glance at Ferenc Szentmarjay. "With you? Where?"

The young man jumped to his feet, "Where? To freedom!

To justice! To destroy everything in this desert and through the ruins toward a new Hungarian life!"

The zaddik shook his head, "We cannot be destroyers here, my son. Even though they chase us, beat us, and drive us to the edge of the village, we are their brothers and we belong to them. We are Hungarians. Our tongues are still unsure. We cannot buy land. We cannot own houses. They bring lawsuits based on superstition against us and they want to slit straps of the skin of our backs. It does not matter. We are Hungarians. Perhaps only in the color of our eyes, perhaps only in the color of our hair, perhaps there is nothing else Hungarian on us but the glow of the Hungarian sun. We are Hungarians just the same. We cannot go with you. We are waiting. Our rights ripen slowly. Our time will arrive belatedly. Our freedom is approaching us through many prisons. We cannot go with you and when I look at you my heart goes out to you."

Ferenc Szentmarjay straightened out in front of the rabbi, "Then farewell, holy man. I feel we'll never speak again. But now we're parting like two men condemned to death. Perhaps the Emperor can save you with a quick order. But nobody can stop me. I am going to victory. Or to death."

Then he lowered his head and said quietly, "Bless me, holy man!"

The zaddik stretched out his hand and touched the young man's forehead. The white light of the May moon broke through the bars. It slid along the zaddik's white hand and rested on the white, powdered wig.

"May my God bless you, Ferenc Szentmarjay," said the zaddik, "your soul will take you on a great and difficult path. Go toward your destiny! But remember: when you will be fighting your great battles with your head raised high, let there be a moment when, like now, you bow your head before God. That is the way you should stand before Heaven after you've been victorious. And that it the way you should stand, humbly and peacefully, should your stiff, stubborn neck bend in front of the executioner."

Ferenc Szentmarjay shuddered. A cool breeze filled the cell. He turned to the rabbi for a last word, "The final questioning will be tomorrow. The trial, the day after."

Then he pulled his cloak over his head and hurried out of the cell with a gloomy face.[45]

What was that "final questioning?"

In Hungary, at the time of the ritual murder trial of Kálló, every kind of questioning by torture had been discontinued for nearly thirty years. It was not allowed to torture the accused. But if he did not want to confess, the "final questioning" was applied.

The court called only three of the principal defendants: the zaddik, Chayyim Weinstein, and Mózsi Oroszlán. The fourth, Reb Shayeh Aaron Fisch, could not be present. He had been sick with fever for five days. They left him in his cell.

The zaddik had not been harmed. His imposing figure made an unusually strong impression on that day. He did not *want* to confess, so they laughed at him. His death sentence was certain, anyway.

Because of his frail health, they did not dare question Reb Chayyim Weinstein forcibly. He was subjected to a different kind of torture. One of the court clerks pulled out a large document that had a seal on it.

"Listen Jew," he said, "if you don't confess we'll have your wife and children jailed. I have just written to Galicia for them."

"You will not jail them, gentlemen," sighed the stranger, "they are not afraid of the court anymore. They lie peacefully in the cemetery of Smihov."

The judges looked at one another. These Jews were obstinate sinners. They had tough, hardened souls. They would surely lie at the trial the next day. But there was a form of inducement until then.

Mózsi Oroszlán, who was thought to be the actual murderer, was made to lie down on a whipping bench after he refused to confess. He got up from it laughing. He did not confess.

When that did not work, they resorted to the final questioning. The "Kálló double." The subprefect issued the order: "Take that bull-backed Jew dancing tonight."

Dancing?

Yes, that was the order. Mózsi Oroszlán was going to dance the Kálló double that night.

The Kálló double is the peasants' dance. Like storks they would lift their feet at weddings in Szabolcs and Hajdú counties. Yet the Kálló double was a dance of Kálló. It had been invented there. At first, however, it was performed not at weddings but in the prison of the county hall.

That dance meant death to many a guilty one. There was a small, narrow cell in the county hall, in the deepest of depths under the cellars. One could not sit down in it. It was equally impossible to stand because its floor was made of pointed iron slabs. The person who was thrown in there had to pick his feet up quickly, or jump up and down, as if he were dancing fast.

That was the famous Kálló double.

Anyone who was put through that bloody entertainment at night became as soft as butter by morning. Everybody confessed after the Kálló double. Even those who had nothing to confess.

When he learned that he would have to "dance" that night, Mózsi Oroszlán shrugged his shoulders and started walking down the steps of the jail, flanked by the zaddik and Reb Chayyim Weinstein and surrounded by armed guards.

Reb Chayyim sighed, "Will anyone avenge our suffering

and our spilled blood? Will anyone make amends for our
sufferings?"

The zaddik looked at him, "There will be someone. If
God allows you to live, you will remain here in our land.
You will have a family and your descendants will remember
your suffering."

They were separated at the entrance of the cellar. Mózsi
Oroszlán looked ahead gloomily. Suddenly the zaddik patted
him on the shoulder.

"Listen, Mózsi," he said in Yiddish so that the guards
would not understand him, "I am telling you this in a
difficult hour: when you see a wagon, get on it whether
or not it has a driver."

Mózsi Oroszlán looked at the zaddik with alarm. Hearing
that meaningless sentence, he thought that the poor soul had
lost his senses in all that harassment. Then the guards surrounded him and took him deeper and deeper underground.
To the deepest cell.

They showed him the way into the cell by the red light
of a torch. Then the door slammed behind him. He was
alone. A crude laughter was heard, and "Good dancing,
Jew!"

"We'll come for you early in the morning," shouted
another. "You can change your mind before then if you
want to confess."

"That is, if you live that long, Mózsi!" sneered a third.

A distant summer storm began to shake the whole castle.
Mózsi Oroszlán shivered in the torture cell. The pointed iron
slabs began their horrible work. He stood on one leg and
then on the other when it became too painful. The cruel
dance began in the gloomy darkness. The Kálló double.

Five yards deep under ground, crushed under the weight
of a terrible, false accusation, suffering innocently alone for
his innocent brothers, and bleeding in the stormy night,
the arms of the Jewish soldier were filled with a terrible
power. The veins swelled on his forehead and his muscles

bulged. His heart ached with the centuries-old bitterness, with every kind of suffering of the oppressed Jewish people. Mózsi Oroszlán bent down. With one grab he yanked out a torturing slab. Then a second. He was breathing hard. At least he was not suffering anymore. He could stand on his feet. Then, with an iron slab in each hand, he threw himself against the dark wall. It yielded. It was made of sandstone. A half hour later, a section of the wall lay in rubble. It could not withstand such powerful arms. Mózsi Oroszlán climbed out of the cell. He was in the cellar of the prison. Outside the storm raged and the wind howled into the cellar. Finally, he found the steps. He ripped out the wooden door easily and stepped out in a large, open square behind the county hall. He looked around as flashes of lightning lit up the night. It must have been around midnight.

A large structure stood directly in front of him. He recognized it by a flash of lightning. It was a wagon with prancing horses in front of it. And in the driver's seat there was no one.

When The Sky Burst

A lonely wagon in the night!

"When you see a wagon, get on it whether or not it has a driver." That was what the zaddik of Kálló said so mysteriously.

Mózsi Oroszlán stood in the large marketplace behind the county hall in the raging storm. His whole body trembled. The guards, or the people of the town could discover his escape in any moment. He lingered but a moment, then jumped on the wagon and hid under the canvas. He had no time to ponder what the zaddik's mysterious words might have meant. As soon as he settled down under the canvas the horses pulled on the wagon and they were off.

They ran with great speed in the lightning-filled night.

Without a driver! The driverless wagon with the wildly running horses cut across the town toward the farms. Mózsi Oroszlán just lay on his stomach on a haystack under the canvas and watched the running horses with amazement. The boards of the wagon squeaked and the joints nearly fell apart as the two horses sped in the night. Where was God taking him, he wondered.

Mózsi Oroszlán began to sense that it was the Creator's hand that had reached down for him in the prison and that it was His mercy that glimmered above his dark fate. His crude, simple soul felt that it was in that night, before the trial on the next day when the fate of the innocently suffering would be decided, that God's mercy was finally turning toward them after so much suffering.

It was difficult to see even a yard ahead in that terrible darkness amid the flashes of lightning and in the icy rain that swept above the fields. The driverless wagon sped along the main highway of Szabolcs. Mózsi Oroszlán could not say which direction it took. At times it appeared to him that they were flying in the air. Indeed, the fields flashed past under their feet and he could see blue and red flames on the hooves of the horses and a silver light that sparkled on their manes.

Were they headed for Balkány[46] or Fehértó?[47] Or were they speeding along the road to Apagy?[48] He tried to peer out, but he saw nothing by the flashes of lightning but the white curtain of hail that covered the fields and the meadows.

Suddenly the wagon stopped with a great jolt. Foam poured off the horses, they seemed to be steaming in sweat. The wagon tilted a little. Someone got on and sat down by Mózsi on the haystack under the canvas.

A stranger.

An old, large-bearded Jew. His moustache and hair were disheveled by the rain and his cape was soaking wet. His kaftan was covered with small white pieces of ice. He held a huge hooked stick in his hand, which he laid alongside him when he sat down. Then the horses set out again. But not as before. They paced with slow, trotting steps as if they were headed for a certain destination.

The old Jew glanced toward Mózsi. But before Mózsi could say a word the old man patted his shoulder and asked, "Do you know what tonight is?"

Mózsi Oroszlán bowed his head. He was filled with a deep feeling of happiness and infinite tranquillity. It did not even occur to him to ask the old man who he was and how he got there, so natural was his appearance in that mysterious night. It was as if his own father were sitting next to him—his father, the old innkeeper, whom he had not seen in two months. Or his grandfather, old Yosef Tégláser, who had died at the age of one hundred the year before. He had had eyes as gentle and hands as warm as the stranger's. Mózsi Oroszlán shook his head and tears rolled down his cheeks; he just did not know what that night was.

"Tonight, my son," the stranger smiled, "is the night of Shovuos."

The night of Shovuos! The night of secrets! Mózsi Oroszlán began to see the light. They were caught after *Pesach* and had been suffering since then. And now Shovuos had arrived, the seven weeks had passed. It was that mysterious night when the old stayed up late by the ancient books, studying, reading, and praying until dawn in preparation for the coming day. For that day was the holiest day of Israel. The day of remembrance for Sinai. That night Jews prepared in their souls for God as did the slaves in Egypt for the great pronouncement. *Lel Shovuos!* The eve of Shovuos! And he broke the holy day on a peasant wagon while his brothers languished in jail.

"Do not cry, my son," the stranger kept smiling, "do not cry. Do you know that tonight every Jew must be engaged in study?"

Mózsi Oroszlán stared at the stranger. Who could he be? His voice was as sweet and mellow as the warm and gentle humming of fire in the oven on a winter evening. Why did every word of the stranger rend his heart? He slid close to him in the darkness.

"*Tatenyu*,"⁴⁹ he begged like a child, "*Tatenyu*, tell me, what shall I do? I can't even study. I know nothing by heart. What should I pray? What should I think on this holy night?"

The old Jew took Mózsi's head between his two hands, as a teacher would do to a bad pupil, and started speaking to him quietly and slowly. "Tonight, you must study and pray. He who does no know how to study anymore should recall only what he had studied at one time. And he who cannot recall anything, might recall certain names, the names of the great and the wise. For on that night even those names become prayers. They rise to Heaven like comets, and shine brightly. But he who cannot recall even names should think of his own poverty, misery, and suffering. His sorrowful thoughts, like the prayers, will also reach God and will beseech Him. Up there, on that night in every year, the large gates open—*chamishim shaare kedusho*, the fifty holy gates, and great brightness pours out through them. It passes from one cloud to the next until it touches both extremities of the firmament. Like over Sinai at one time, the sky bursts for a moment."

"The sky bursts," repeated Mózsi Oroszlán in a daze, "and all of our wishes are granted."

The stranger got up from the haystack and sat in the driver's seat. Mózsi could feel by the gradually increasing pace of the horses that they had reached the marshes. The stranger grabbed the reins and the horses slowed down to an easy pace in the dark. Suddenly the wagon stopped. Mózsi Oroszlán moved into the driver's seat, next to the stranger. He looked around inquisitively in the darkness. Where could they be?

The rain and hail subsided and the wind calmed down. There was heavy silence in the humid air. The stranger raised his eyes to the sky as if he prayed. Suddenly a yellow light lit up the sky. It shot across on a zigzag line like a flash of lightning. The clouds parted in its path. It moved westward, setting the whole firmament ablaze, and in one terrible flash of lightning the dark night gave way to the clearness of the day. It was light.

And then . . . the sky burst!

Mózsi Oroszlán's heart was beating fast as he looked around. They must be near the Tisza. And among the marshes and tussocks. hardly ten feet from the wagon, a small hut became visible in the bright light. There were many small ponds and seaweed-covered islets in the marshes, and the hut itself stood on one of the islets. An old peasant stood in front of it in the rain, leaning on his cane and with a pipe in his mouth. A Tisza fisherman. Like a statue, he stood there motionless.

The huge flash of lightning disappeared. In the sky the clouds merged and it was dark again. Only the peasant's pipe kept smoldering in the dark. A deep, serious voice rang out, "Did you come for the Kálló girl?"

Mózsi Oroszlán suddenly realized what was happening. He jumped off the wagon and walked up to the fisherman. "Where is the girl?" he asked.

"She's asleep in the shack. I've been waiting for about four weeks for someone to fetch her. I found her in the marshes and had to drag her out of the seaweed. Probably she ran away from home in her grief. She didn't want to send a message home, the stubborn soul, and she said they would come for her if they missed her. Since then she has been here helping me with the fishing, but she is missing her folks a lot."

Mózsi stuck his head into the hut. He saw nothing but a white dress. He recognized it at once. It belonged to Forget-Me-Not. She was wearing that dress when she ran away after his kiss. "Let's hurry," he said to the fisherman, "place her on the wagon without waking her. And then you'll come with us, too. You'll get a reward from the law."

Forget-Me-Not was sleeping soundly. She did not awaken

when she was placed on the soft pile of hay. The old
fisherman squatted next to her. Mózsi Oroszlán and the
old Jew sat in the driver's seat.

The horses paced briskly. The day was breaking in the
east after the stormy night. The clouds started scattering.
Mózsi hoped to reach Kálló by noon.

The stranger, sitting next to him, just kept smiling.
Mózsi turned to him. "What a holiday, *Tatenyu* . . . What a
dawn . . . What a Shovuos . . ."

The old man patted him on the face. "Stop the horses,
my son," he said, "I am getting off."

The wagon stopped. The stranger got off, shook Mózsi's
hand and smiled. "You will find the way home, won't you?"
he asked. "Just keep to the right and you will reach home
by noon."

Only Mózsi's eyes dared to ask the silent question, "Why
won't you come along?"

The stranger held Mózsi's hand firmly. "I have a great
deal to do today, my son," he responded. "It is a holiday.
There is a great deal of trouble and suffering, and in the
synagogues many thousands of hearts are turned sorrowfully
toward the Lord. Israel is in danger everywhere. I have
already helped you. Many people are keeping awake on
this night, and their prayers must be led before the Throne.
There are many decisions that must be changed. My people
are celebrating a holiday on this day and I must make sure
that it is a happy one. I must ensure peace for Israel." And
he was off in the dark.

Mózsi looked after him bewildered. Some miraculous
realization burst forth from his soul. Those childhood tales.
. . . And he stood up in the driver's seat and shouted, *"Elye
nove! Elye nove!"*[50] But he could see nothing of the stranger
except an uncertain silvery light that fluttered as it receded

above the steppe of Szabolcs. The prophet disappeared in the distance.

At the same time, a great noise and the rumble of wheels were heard on the highway. A large yellow carriage, led by outriders, was passing by Mózsi's wagon. Through its mirrorlike windows an elegant officer could be seen asleep, leaning back on pillows. "The Emperor's courier! The Emperor's courier!" the outriders yelled at Mózsi. "Off with your wagon!"

Mózsi cleared out of the way. He allowed the imperial courier's carriage to pass him. It sped on in the direction of Kálló.

Mózsi's wagon moved slowly, and he started brooding in the driver's seat in the early morning light: "It was *Elye nove*. He came like the fog and he left like the fog. His voice was just like my father's. What he said was like music to my ears. I didn't even understand it. But it was he who sent this wagon to my prison, it was he who got on it at the turn, and it was he who guided it through the treacherous marshes. And I kept awake with him on that holy night and I was one of the pious, too. The zaddik of Kálló knew all of this in advance. But I don't understand it even now. And who is going to believe me when I tell him of this unusual night or of the sky bursting above us at his prayer?"

Emperor Joseph's courier, Colonel Damonville, arrived in Kálló at eleven o'clock in the morning. He asked for the prefect. He was escorted into the courtroom of the county hall. The trial of the ritual murder accusation was already in progress. He was made to wait a whole hour before he was admitted before the court. He passed along the row of benches and the column of bound Jewish defendants. He pulled out a letter from his coat and handed it over to the prefect. "His Majesty's order," he said in German.

The prefect shrugged his shoulders and passed the letter to the subprefect. The eyes of the subprefect, Kállay, flashed

in anger when he opened the emperor's order. He read it
silently, but as he neared its end he continued reading aloud
so that the judges could hear it too," . . . and that We forbid
the county the prolonged preoccupation with that senseless
accusation which belongs to the Middle Ages. The lost girl
is to be searched for for three months and the imprisoned
Jews are to be released on this day until the conclusion of
the investigation.

At Lugos, anno 1789.

Josephus, Imperator."

The subprefect's face turned red. The members of the
county court jumped to their feet. "He has offended the
county again, dammit!" they shouted. The subprefect,
shaking the letter, addressed the colonel from the rostrum:
"The county court obeys only the county, Colonel. No one
else. The Emperor cannot free murderers just because they
happen to be of his favorite Jews. Tell His Majesty,
Colonel . . ."

Suddenly great commotion was heard outside. Shouts
went up from the crowd in front of the county hall. The
subprefect dropped the letter and stared at the door. The
huge door of the county court opened slowly. In the middle
of a large, inrushing group of people Mózsi Oroszlán stood
with a victorious expression on his face. Next to him, stood
the old fisherman, holding his worn hat. And in front of
them, wearing a torn white dress and with a flaming red
face and downcast eyes, stood Forget-Me-Not, the innkeeper's blue-eyed daughter.

"We've brought her home, Mr. Subprefect," thundered
Mózsi Oroszlán.

Reb Chayyim Weinstein recovered from the effects of
the prison in a few months. He bade farewell to the zaddik
of Kálló, who gave him a letter of introduction to Tura.[51]
The Jews of that village were looking for a cantor. So, Reb

Chayyim Weinstein set out for Tura on a fine summer afternoon. He had nothing but the zaddik's letter in his pocket, some provisions, a cane in his hand, and his voice, on his way toward a new life. But Reb Chayyim Weinstein was satisfied with what he had. The sun shone brightly and the sky was clear. He felt that the curse that had followed him had now disappeared. Satan had drawn back humiliated from his side. Satan could not tempt him, for he remained faithful to God even in suffering. The curse was ended; only blessing could follow it. The zaddik had even spoken of an upright widow who lived in Tura and could be his wife for many a happy year.

Reb Chayyim Weinstein started singing on the road. He sang of God, whose power is infinite and whose mercy is eternal; of the people of Israel, who had to suffer so much but who were the happiest of peoples because God was theirs; and of happiness, that great, miraculous, Jewish happiness that radiated from God. Of happiness that lasts forever.

7

The Market of Debrecen

Reb Chayyim Weinstein started his long journey on a horse-drawn wagon from the town of Tiszafüred at four o'clock in the morning. It was a bitterly cold and windy morning; small snowflakes were flying through the air. The morning dew descended like a carpet of white smoke, and Reb Chayyim trembled and quivered in the driver's seat. He had never been so cold as he was on that day.

Basically, however, he was surprised that he was cold. After all, he had performed his morning prayers, and that by itself should set one's soul and body afire. He drank his customary morning brandy, which usually ignited small furnaces in him. He recited the most beautiful psalms, which never failed to set the heart afire and fill the brain with warmth. Still, he was cold. As he sat in the driver's seat surrounded by the cold breath of dawn, he was getting colder and colder. He was tortured by shivering and his knees kept knocking against each other. Such a thing had never happened to Reb Chayyim, and he began to examine himself with justifiable curiosity and amazement, "What can be wrong with me?"

The two horses trotted briskly on the road made hard by the morning freeze, and the first snowflakes of the winter playfully flew around the fur collar of Reb Chayyim's coat. "Why am I so cold?" he asked the trees that turned up in front of his wagon.

He touched them as he passed by them. And the trees asked him in return, "Have you sinned?"

"No."

"Then where are you traveling in such a hurry?"

"To the market of Debrecen."

"Do you want to do big business there?"

"No, I just want to make a living," replied Reb Chayyim, "enough for my family to live on."

"And what will you sell at the market?"

"What will I sell? Fish . . . fish, because today is Friday and on that day Jews buy fish for the Sabbath."

"There are perhaps sinful thoughts or desires inside you," the trees persisted.

"No, no," he protested, "I love the Lord, the Torah, the world around us, my family, and I am looking forward to the coming of the Messiah. I am pure; pure and sinless."

And with this the secret discussion between Reb Chayyim and the trees ended. The cold and shivers, however, continued. The red-faced winter sun had already risen above the steppe and the small villages through which Reb Chayyim's wagon passed amid the sound of church bells. It was morning everywhere, but Reb Chayyim got colder and colder. He leaned forward in his seat, sank into his thoughts, and reflected upon the smallest detail of his life. Nothing helped; he was still very, very cold. No doubt about it, he was in for something extraordinary. He was either going to be ill, something miraculous was going to happen to him, or he was going to strike it rich. Perhaps fate was not going to favor him alone. Perhaps it was going to be a great day for all of Israel. That's what his trembling body was trying to tell him! Perhaps he was about to hear and see things by which slavery would end and all Jews would be liberated and would not have to suffer or serve others anymore. "Perhaps that is why I am so cold," murmured Reb Chayyim with quivering lips.

The wagon came to a halt with a sudden jolt at the

customs house of Debrecen. Two imperial customs officials lifted the canvas off the wagon, reached into the large bucket, and grabbed at some of the fishes. Having found nothing illegal, they smacked Reb Chayyim in the back. "Drive on, Jew." And the cart slowly rode into the city of Debrecen. Gradually driving became difficult. Reb Chayyim stood up to steer his horses in the right direction. Their progress was slow amid the numerous wagons. The burghers, smoking big pipes, swarmed among the wagons and the merchants had already begun to sell their goods. To escape the crowd of cursing butcher apprentices and petty vendors, Reb Chayyim made a sudden decision before he reached the market. He steered his horses into a narrow side street and brought them to a halt in front of a small, single-storied house.

There were already about ten Jews standing by the door. Inside, the accustomed sounds of the morning prayer filled the air—a mournful and protracted song suddenly interrupted by joyous clapping and exuberant voices. It was in this small synagogue that Reb Chayyim liked to pray when he came to Debrecen. The zaddik of Olaszliszka[2] and the zaddik of Ujfehértó[3] frequented the synagogue when their business brought them to the city. There were always a few zaddikim who traveled between Ujhely[4] and Nagyvárad[5] and hoped to find someone with whom to spend time in enjoyable discussion. Perhaps he would also be rid of the shivering cold that had been torturing him all morning. But before he could bring his wagon to a halt and descend from the driver's seat, someone ran to him from the small gathering in front of the synagogue and said, "Reb Chayyim! What are you doing in Debrecen?"

Reb Chayyim recognized the man. It was Reb Zese, who used to live in his home town but had come to live in Debrecen the month before. He jumped on the driver's seat. "You've come to the market, haven't you?"

"Yes, Reb Zese, to the market. And how are you doing here?"

Reb Zese shrugged his shoulders, "Every morning I pray for our daily bread, and then our Lord, may His name be praised in His infinite kindness, provides us with sustenance. He who provides food for the Leviathan, for every lizard and for every butterfly will provide for me too when I call for help to Him. But don't go yet, Reb Chayyim, let me tell you what we have been talking about in secret." He leaned over and whispered into Reb Chayyim's ear, "They say *he* is here in Debrecen."

"Who . . . who is here?" asked Reb Chayyim somewhat alarmed.

"The prophet Elijah."

Reb Chayyim just stared into the cold air and his hands started to tremble. "Who saw him?"

"Last night someone knocked on the window of the *shammes's*[6] house," whispered Reb Zese. "The *shammes* looked out and saw a stranger, wearing a large, wide-brimmed hat, who shouted at him to run to the synagogue because some people were about to set it on fire. The *shammes* ran to the synagogue just in time. Its roof was already smoking. With the help of others, the *shammes* smothered the smoke. But no one knew who the stranger was."

Reb Chayyim just stared into the air and sighed. "Tell me more."

"There is more," continued Reb Zese. "Last night someone knocked on the door of a woman who was still in bed following her child's birth. It was a stranger wearing a large hat and carrying firewood on his shoulders. The poor woman had been shivering in the cold room and told the stranger that she had no money to warm her room. The stranger entered nonetheless, made a fire, left two *thalers*[7] on the table, and disappeared."

"Is there more?" trembled Reb Chayyim.

"Yes, there is more. This morning during the service, a boy from Vámospércs[8] burst into the synagogue. His mother was sick, he said, and he had come to Debrecen for the doctor. In front of the customs house, however, two youths attacked him and started beating him. They wanted to push him into the snow so that he would suffocate, but suddenly a stranger, wearing a wide cape and a large hat, appeared. He just swished his cape and the two youths fell to the ground. The stranger lifted the boy in his arms and carried him into the city."

"Yes, it is he," sighed Reb Chayyim in relief.

Having disclosed his secret, Reb Zese quickly took his leave of Reb Chayyim and jumped off the driver's seat. He put his forefinger across his lips, "But don't talk about this to anyone."

Of course. We cannot discuss this with anyone. This is a secret to be divulged only among the faithful. It must remain the secret of souls. But how do you silence the heart, the brain? The heart starts to beat faster of joy, the eyes are filled with tears of happiness, and the brain forms wonderful tales. The soul is rekindled in the body, like a light in the tunnel, and grows stronger by the approaching great brightness. The prophet is here, the millennial guest! Like a comet that appears on the horizon, moves across the sky followed by its silvery train, and disappears. The prophet is here in the darkness of oppression, in the night of servitude; the burning comet, the exalted guest, the friend of the poor, the healer of the sick, the scourge of the evil, Israel's friend.

"What a day," reflected Reb Chayyim, "and what hours! This secret is ours, a few initiated ones; the others around me, all unbelievers and ignorant, know nothing of it. Only I know him, only I shall see him, because I am one of his people. And all of you around me know nothing, nothing. . . ."

Reb Chayyim got a rather modest place at the market of Debrecen. In the seventh row, behind the tents of the potters and glaziers. He unfolded his small canvas, lifted his bucket off the wagon, and was ready to sell his fish. He filled his pipe, sat down on at empty box, and waited.

The crowd swarmed around him, but no one came to buy

from him. But Reb Chayyim was far from being concerned.
His buyers usually came after ten o'clock—old Jewish women,
quarreling cooks, and careful old men who bought fish for
the Sabbath. They were sure buyers. He did not need to
make himself conspicuous or to offer his fish for sale in a
loud voice; all of them came looking for him and they found
him, even if by chance he was assigned to the last row. And
they were glad to buy from him. After all, was it not true that
he was doing them a favor by purchasing fish from the fishermen and bringing them to the market? On that day, as usual,
they would snap up all ten of them. Yes, there were only ten:
five carps, three pikes, and two small fish from the Tisza.
How lively they were, how happy! The carps swam slowly
and with dignity, whereas the pikes moved with greater speed.
The two Tisza fish, howeverd, appeared almost lifeless, moving only from time to time when the others pushed them and
kept staring at Reb Chayyim with their eyes, those immobile,
silent, and mysterious fish eyes. What did they want of him?
Why did they stare at him so? Was there something of a
hidden reproach, a terrible accusation in those fish eyes staring at him, who made his living by sending those creatures
to their deaths? Was he allowed to do that? Was life no
happiness for those creatures? Did they not like the sun
and brightness? Did they not deserve enjoyment and happiness? And did they not have something behind those eyes?
Something that no one knew, perhaps only suspected: some
mystery or another form of life?

Reb Chayyim shuddered at these thoughts. Yet it was
not the first time that these thoughts occurred to him. Ever
since he became a seller of fish, two years before, he
experienced the unhappiest moments of his life every week
when the time came to sell his fish. When he had to face the
unfortunate creatures, to endure their sad look, and to think
that—God forbid!—a wandering soul could be hiding in one
of them. A wandering soul, which had sinned in its earthly
life and up there it was sentenced to start a new life in the

body of such a meek creature. What a terrible fate! What a shocking thought! And what about the story that the zaddik of Fehértó[9] had told about a certain fish that cried out when it was cut in half because a living soul had been hiding inside it and that, like a dead man, was buried in the Jewish cemetery of Vienna? Even a tombstone was erected over the grave.

At that moment a shadow fell on the fish bucket. Reb Chayyim looked up: a stranger stood in front of him.

A large black cape on which small snowflakes glittered. A wide-brimmed black hat. In his hand a huge cane, like the ones the shepherds carried in the steppe. And his eyes—

"Greetings, Reb Chayyim," said the stranger.

Reb Chayyim could not answer. He just stared at the stranger's eyes. What fire, what blue flame blazing in those eyes! And his beard, in which silvery streaks glittered with unusual intensity.

"Greetings, Reb Chayyim," said the stranger again.

Reb Chayyim was still too dazed to answer. Who could this man be? How was it that he knew his name? Or did he know him? But how . . . from where? In his dreams? Was he the one who seemed to appear to him in the dark corner of the synagogue on the feverish night of the Day of Atonement?

"Greetings, Reb Chayyim," said the stranger for the third time, and smiled.

Reb Chayyim felt his heart sink. He held his breath. Suddenly he started to tremble. The shivers were the same as those he had endured on the seat of his wagon at dawn. His knees kept knocking against each other. *He is here!* It is he! Face to face! And he, Reb Chayyim Weinstein, lived to see that. That he might see him, the invisible one, who destroyed the altars of Baal, rode to Heaven in a fiery chariot and was Akiba's friend!

Reb Chayyim lowered his head, "May your arrival be blessed, my lord."

The stranger smiled. He firmly planted his cane against the ground and quickly asked, "Have you any wishes, Reb Chayyim?"

Reb Chayyim straightened up. This was the moment! Now he could wish for anything. A once-in-a-lifetime opportunity. He could wish for money, a hundred thousand *thalers*, all at once. But what for? Wealth could lead to disaster. His children would frown at honest work and cease to be observing Jews. He could wish for health and long life. But what for? He was fifty-six years old already, the Lord would perhaps grant him another ten to twenty years, and beyond that, why bother? Why should a man outlive his usefulness and become a burden to others? Still, he could wish for palaces, kingdoms, empires, and fortified castles; for ships, carriages, a garden with a fountain, and bejeweled royal ladies. What's the use? What would he do with all that, he, a kaftaned simple Jew, Reb Chayyim Weinstein from Tiszafüred?

He slowly unfolded his hands, which had been tightly squeezed together as if to grasp in one moment all the riches of the world. He released his dreams, his desires, all of his wishes. And he answered the stranger quietly, "No my lord, I have no wishes."

The stranger nodded his head and something of an encouraging light, like the friendly fire of a furnace in the depth of a wintry forest, lit up in his eyes. And in that deep, resounding, and melodic voice, he spoke again, "As you wish, Reb Chayyim. I am glad to hear that you are satisfied with your lot. I could not have given you greater happiness. But think it over; perhaps I could still do something for you. Have you not been afraid to divulge a wish hidden in your heart?"

Reb Chayyim lowered his eyes. Then he looked over the crowded, noisy market where thousands of people were swarming and crowding, not even suspecting who was among them and what the two men in the last row of tents were discussing. Finally his eyes wandered over to his bucket and he said, "Please, my lord, buy my fish."

The stranger looked at him, "Is yours a difficult occupation, Reb Chayyim?"

"Yes, my lord, very difficult."

"I shall buy your fish, Reb Chayyim."

"Thank you, my lord."

"And what are you going to do now, Reb Chayyim, that you have sold your fish?"

"I shall go home to my family two hours earlier than otherwise. Tomorrow is Sabbath, my lord."

The stranger pulled on his cape. He opened his hand: there were pieces of gold glittering in it. He looked into the bucket and threw the gold pieces into it. Then he turned and disappeared.

Reb Chayyim ran after him, but the stranger was faster. "The fish, my lord, the fish!" shouted Reb Chayyim. "You have bought the fish and left them here."

The stranger's large black hat floated farther and farther away in the swarming sea of the market. Here and there it stopped in front of a Jew's tent. Then it disappeared again only to reappear at some tattered tent as if its owner wanted to talk to every Jewish merchant, as if he had brought a message to each one of them. But did they know to whom they were talking? Did they sense who came to visit them? Did they recognize him? If only Reb Chayyim could run and tell everyone that he was here . . . here at the market of Debrecen.

Reb Chayyim remained alone with his fish. Loud and happy sounds were heard coming from the bucket. The carps and the pikes were rejoicing and giving thanks for their lives. Reb Chayyim cast a distant look toward them and reached into the bucket for the gold pieces. He found three gold pieces, three gold *thalers*—as much as he would earn in half a year.

"You are no longer mine," said Reb Chayyim to the fish

quietly, "I have sold you. But since you have been left here, I shall take you back to the Tisza. The Lord spared me from selling you so that I might earn my food for the Sabbath. The Lord gave me life, and I cannot take yours. The Lord worked wonders with me, and I shall do with you likewise. Do not be afraid, God's creatures; do not look at me angrily! I shall take you back to your home, as I shall return home to my children."

With that he lifted the bucket and placed it on the wagon. Then he climbed on the seat and swished his whip over the horses.

"Is there no market, Jew?" shouted a young potter's apprentice at him. "Where are you taking your fish?"

"The market is over for me, son. I have sold what I had and received what was due me. And now I am taking the fish back to the Tisza."

The young man burst into laughter and good-naturedly pulled on Reb Chayyim's kaftan. Reb Chayyim, however, kept a serious face and steered his horses, through the sea of merchants hurrying out of the crowded town, toward the road leading to Tiszafüred. When he was out of the city, he lit his pipe and smoothed his beard. "Could I be richer?" he asked himself. "After all, what happened to me is no big thing, yet still a miracle. There are big miracles and there are small miracles. I have earned my daily bread and in doing that I did not have to do anyone wrong. I have got my daily bread, yet I did not have to destroy anyone for it. Of course, there are people who have more money than I. But has anyone had a day more beautiful than this day has been for me?"

And having said that, he squinted as he looked up toward the sky where the sun emerged from the snowy clouds of November.

8

The Wedding of Levelek[1]

The Proposal

The zaddik of Kálló had been working in his village for two years when a messenger arrived on a pleasant spring night from Poland, or perhaps even farther.

The young rebbe of Kálló was busy telling stories to his faithful, who sat around him piously on a bench in his moonlit courtyard. The stories were about the great zaddikim and the old Kabbalists, of Chayyim Vital and the fanatical Yitzhak Luria. After all, no one had ever spoken of these heroes of the Kabbalah in the Hungarian language as did the zaddik. He spoke Hungarian excellently, which was not suprising, for he was a Hungarian by birth, a shepherd boy before his parents put him into the *cheder*[2] and before he went on the accustomed wanderings of Talmudists, which led through Galicia to Poland.

Anyway, there was Reb Eizik with his disciples, who listened delightedly as he spoke about the origin of the *Zohar,* the most important book of the Kabbalah, which, as the rebbe alleged, was written by an ill-fated Talmudist, Rabbi Simon ben Yochai, in the thirteen years while he was hiding from the Romans in a cave. The story rolled on quietly, at times interrupted by songs for the rebbe loved to sing. And the disciples listened to the young master en-

chantedly as he struck up the rousing hymn of the Kabbalists, which Chayyim Vital had composed in the hot East
about the eternal longing of God and Israel for each other.
And the sweet melody rang out in the quiet of the night:

> *Daydi yurad legannai liyras bagannim*
> *Lishtashshea velikayt shoyshannim;*
> *Kayl daydi dayfek: pischi li tammosi*
> *Shaare Ziyayn asher ohovosi.*

In that love poem, God is the lover and Israel is the
scattered, persecuted Israel. His poor people, after whom He
is longing. The Kabbalist poet borrowed his rhymes from
the Song of Songs. The lover, the poem says, goes down in
his garden to pick roses and lilies. And he knocks on his
lover's door—"open it my sweet, open the beloved gates of
Zion for me."

Deep, thousand-year-old suffering filled the song. To find
God again and to return to Zion—the song went on, the
dream flew farther, and tears filled the corners of the weary
eyes. What an eternal, powerful desire! It could never be
torn out of Jewish hearts. It would remain there forever.
And the rebbe continued his song. In that verse God turned
consolingly toward a despairing Israel:

> *Bitti, al tifchadi, ki ayd ezkorech*
> *Umeeretz rechayko akkabetz pezurech*
> *Ayd evnech venivnes beyofyech vehadurech*
> *Vegam omnom att achaysi.*

Do not fear, my daughter! For I shall remember you,
from the four corners of the earth I shall gather you together.
I shall rebuild you and you shall be rebuilt beautifully and
triumphantly. After all, you are my sister, my beloved sister,
you beautiful Israel.

How much sadness, hopelessness, and futile yearning!
The singing stopped at that verse and sad, tearful Jewish
faces turned toward the sky—above the steppe of Szabolcs
the nights were so clear—where the stars revolved in perpetual

tranquillity. How blue and clear were those shimmering little sparks in the spring sky! But if the Kabbalists' eyes looked at them, they would search for the invisible spheres beyond them—spheres woven of silvery nets, shimmering beyond the nest of the stars, spheres with their golden suns, mysterious heavenly music whose heights only the *Zohar*, the God-searching holy book knows. But the Jewish eyes find beauty not in the stars but in God, whose small lanterns they are; not in the clearness of the sky, but in the throne of the Lord whose blue texture it forms.

The stamping of hooves and the clatter of a wagon interrupted the midnight silence. The idyllic picture disappeared. A visitor had come to the rebbe. Who could it be so late?

When a servant lifted his lantern to the visitor's face, excited whispering started in the rebbe's courtyard. "Reb Leib Sarahs!"

Reb Leib Sarahs was a great name in the world of the pious. He was none other than the majordomo of the Baal-Shem. He had been a zaddik himself in Poland, but left his village in order to become a servant of the Baal-Shem in Podolia. What kind of message could Reb Leib Sarahs have brought from the Baal-Shem? What could be the purpose of his coming? What news did the sun have for the little star, the old master for the youthful disciple?

He brought sad news. He handed a sealed letter to the zaddik of Kálló. The latter read it by the flickering light of the lantern. His face turned serious, his eyes closed, and his lips moved in silent prayer. He let out a big, deep sigh, then hurried into the house, packed some food and a few pieces of clothing, and got on the wagon next to Reb Leib Sarahs. His faithful stood by the wagon bewildered. They had no idea where their master was going. And when the driver had already struck his whip between the horses, the rebbe turned back and said, "Say the *tillem.*"

To recite the psalms was customary only for the recovery

of the gravely ill. "For God's sake, not the Baal-Shem!" thought the faithful, trembling.

Yes, it was as they thought. The great Baal-Shem was lying on his deathbed in Myedziborz, Podolia. His disciples, students, and admirers stood around him. The signs of great pain could be seen on his pale face. His white and withered hands, like lilies broken off, rested on a pillow. Crying and wailing filled the room, but the pious man just smiled.

"Don't cry, Rebboysem," he said. "What is happening to me? What is death? I shall step out through one door and step in through another so I may find beauty in God's radiance."

The true hasid is not afraid of death. In fact, he prepares for it as if it were a holiday, a joyous occasion. He calls death *hillula* or wedding, when the liberated soul joins God in a wedding ceremony. What is immortal in man meets Heaven. And the Baal-Shem waited for the arrival of death, smiling.

Only when he looked at the small boy who stood quietly by his bed did his face turn serious. He had fine features and blond hair, and wore a velvet suit. The great Baal-Shem anxiously touched the boy's forehead.

"Look outside," he said from time to time, "isn't the Kalever coming yet?"

It was the afternoon before Shovuos—when the synagogue is decorated and roses on the curtains covering the ark release their fragrance—that the rabbi of Kálló arrived at the sickbed. The Baal-Shem ordered everyone out of the room. His fever-ridden countenance brightened; he shook the hands of Reb Eizik of Kálló with both hands and remained in secret discussion with him for an hour.

No one knew what they discussed. Everyone in the house, the courtyard, the street, the whole village spoke of nothing but of that secret discussion, without even guessing its topic. It was surely not a trifling thing for which the master just before his death summoned his young pupil from a faraway land.

When Reb Eizik of Kálló came out of the room of the Baal-Shem, he appeared to have gone through a remarkable change. His sad face was shining and his high forehead radiated pride and consciousness like a man who had been entrusted with a great, important mission that was to occupy his whole life. He held a prayer book in his hands, the large, brown book of Psalms of the Baal-Shem, which the master himself had copied with his pearl-like letters in that hut in the Carpathian Mountains where he had prepared for his mission in mysterious solitude.

And the rabbi of Kálló stood by the bed of the Baal-Shem with his face bearing the same expression of pride and joy on the following day, on the holy day of Shovuos, when that great man returned his soul to God—with a faint smile on his lips, quietly applauding, and looking at some distant, invisible fire that reflected in his wide-open eyes.

The Baal-Shem died surrounded by God's eternal love, like Rabbi Chanina ben Teradyon on the stake, like the martyrs in a Roman circus and at the hands of the executioners of the Inquisition.

The rabbi of Kálló returned to his village following that notable festival of Shovuos. He carried the holy prayer book under his arm and on the wagon next to him sat the little boy whom the Baal-Shem had entrusted to him. The boy's name was Yisroel.

Ten years passed.

Many things change in ten years. Tender plants grow up to make forests, shrubs thicken into bushes, and dry poplars burst into bloom on the hot banks of the Tisza. In ten years even the unusual aloe opens its lazy bell in the murky, warm-water puddles by the highway of Kálló.

In ten years, little Yisroel, who had been brought there from a distant land, had grown up in the house of the zaddik of Kálló. He was looked after with great care. He studied day and night—could it be otherwise in a famous rabbi's house?—but his life was different from that of the other Talmudists. He was dressed in velvet and silk, and gentle fingers combed his blond locks. He received a damask-colored festive kaftan and a black fur *spodek*[3] in which he looked like a Polish prince. He was forbidden to mingle with the common people or with the strangers who came in an uninterrupted flow. He slept in the rebbe's room, and no Jewish boy in the province had a better lot than he.

The Jews of the village, who had at first been excited and curious, calmed down gradually. They surrounded the little stranger with timid respect. The rebbe would not answer their frequent questions as to whose son little Yisroel was. Finally most of the curious ones reconciled themselves to the idea that gained general acceptance, that the rebbe was bringing up an orphan in his house—for they believed that the Baal-Shem had no son—for whom the Baal-Shem had provided previously.

The rabbi of Kálló had no children (later, in the beginning of the nineteenth century, a son was born to him whom he named Mayerl i.e., Meir). But in those ten years the rabbi of Kálló acquired rather strange habits. He would leave his house at dawn to seek the company of simple farm folk, and after sunset he was seen sitting with shepherds by their campfire. At night he took long rides on the wagon to neighboring villages. He drove the horses himself, but on one of his trips he was accompanied by a disciple hidden behind the seat in great secrecy. On the following day, trembling, he described the miraculous things that happened to the rebbe's wagon. They flew over counties in minutes and the rebbe descended on strange cities and villages and questioned their inhabitants thoroughly. But about whom, the hasid who stole away in the wagon could not say.

What was the rebbe looking for? What was he searching for among the farms and villages, at the campfires and in his nightly journeys?

No one knew.

This went on day after day, night after night, and the rebbe became sadder and paler. His good humor left him. He could not even sing his favorite song, "The Cock is Crowing Already," which he had learned from a shepherd on the meadow (the shepherd was none other than the prophet Elijah). He often read in that big book of Psalms, that the Baal-Shem had given him as a gift, and one of his followers noticed that he wrote a strange prayer on the first page of the book. It went like this:

"*Yechi rotzon milfonecho* . . . May Thy will be realized, o God, God of my fathers, God of my ancestors, that all the suffering which Thou hast willed upon Thy people. Israel may come upon me; that all trouble destined to inflict them may inflict me; that all sickness ordered to plague them may torture me. That this may be Thy will, Amen."

It was the prayer of a sad, dejected, and maladjusted soul!

One day—just before Shovuos, exactly ten years after the death of the Baal-Shem—the zaddik of Kálló called for Reb Shayeh Aaron Fisch, his most trusted man, and asked him to prepare the wagon and bring it to him at one o'clock in the morning.

They drove out of the village at night, by the bright light of the moon, straight toward the steppes. As they passed by his farm Reb Shayeh Aaron Fisch noticed something glittering like silver. He was astonished when he saw that it was a small lake, although not a drop of water was to be found on his farm. The rebbe smiled, got off the wagon, and bathed in the warm water of the new lake on the night of the anniversary. It was like bathing before praying. And he explained to Reb Shayeh Aaron that the mirage was nothing else but the well of the wandering Miryam of the Bible, whose water had for thousands of years been sprouting forth here and there for a few moments. When they resumed their journey, the rebbe said to the dumbfounded Reb Shayeh

Aaron Fisch, "That lake was certainly a good omen for tonight."

Reb Aaron Fisch was speechless.

The wagon moved quietly on the moonlit highway. The rebbe handed over the reins to Reb Shayeh Aaron Fisch, stood up in the driver's seat, and looked ahead in the direction of the road as if waiting, searching for someone. At one of the turns, the horses came to a sudden stop. Quite unexpectedly, a man stood in front of the wagon.

Reb Shayeh Aaron Fisch, who later told this story to his children, alleged that the man was a Jew wearing a shabby kaftan. At first, when he saw the man's smiling face emerging from the darkness suddenly and mysteriously, he thought that it was a *letz*.[4] But then he took a good look. It was certainly no *letz*. He had kind features, a long, silvery beard, and bushy eyebrows. He held a huge stick in his hand and his coat had many patches on it. The man was surely a simple *forer*, a traveling, wandering rabbi—a kind of second-class wonder-worker who, because people would not come to him, went to the people from village to village; a *forer* whose large family and misery forced him to wander even at night. That is what Reb Shayeh Aaron Fisch thought of the man.

But the rebbe thought otherwise. As if he had been struck by lightning, he jumped off the wagon, overjoyed. He ran to the stranger, kissed the hem of his kaftan, and threw himself at his feet. The stranger lifted up the rabbi of Kálló, kissed him on his forehead, and whispered something in his ear. And then he pointed with his stick toward the distant peasant houses where the people of the village of Levelek slept in their white homes in the darkness of night. With that he embraced the rabbi of Kálló again and disappeared.

As the man disappeared, Reb Shayeh Aaron knew at once that it was neither an elf, nor a rabbi, nor a wanderer, but *Elye nove,* the prophet Elijah himself, who had stood in front of them on the highway of Levelek.

The rebbe jumped on the driver's seat happily, grabbed the reins, and turned the wagon around. The horses started to plod toward Levelek.

On the road there, the frightened Reb Shayeh Aaron asked some questions but received no reply.

It was broad daylight when they reached Levelek. They drove along the main street. The wagon stopped in front of the synagogue (it was a small room in the house of a Jew named Landauer). The Jews were just getting out following the morning prayer. There was great commotion among them, "The Kalever! The rabbi of Kálló has come to Levelek."

They crowded around the wagon happily as they tried to touch his clothes. Reb Shayeh Aaron Fisch sat proudly in the driver's seat, although he had no idea what in the world they were looking for in Levelek. The rabbi of Kálló patiently endured the crowd's display of affection and then quietly said, "Now, my friends, where does Reb Dov Wasserschepper live? I've come to visit him."

The crowd—if fifteen to twenty Jews can be called a crowd—rumbled and surged. Reb Dov Wasserschepper! The last man in the village! He was the attendant at the well of the village, in front of the blacksmith's shop, from which came his name of water carrier (*Wasserschöpfer*). He prepared the water for the horses of wagon drivers and for the returning herd. Did the famous rabbi come to visit that man? What could be the meaning of this?

When the rebbe learned the whereabouts of the watering Jew (everyone in the village called him that), he cracked his whip and the wagon rumbled through the village. They stopped at the last house. There was a large draw well on the meadow and a heavy-bearded, disheveled Jew was working on one of its arms.

"Reb Dov!" shouted the rebbe. "We've come to ask you for your daughter's hand for my foster son."

Reb Dov grumbled something to the effect that they should leave him alone and not make fun of him. But the rebbe took him by the arm and the three of them walked into Reb Dov's house.

It was indeed a sad little house. A large earthenware oven filled the room almost completely. It was the place where cooking was done; it also provided heat and served as a repository of seeds.

"Where is your daughter?" the rebbe asked Reb Dov and his unkempt wife, whose hands were covered with dough that she had been kneading and who was staring at the guests with open mouth.

"My daughter," responded Reb Dov angrily, "is sitting on the bench upstairs. She can't come down because she hasn't got a decent dress. She is still wearing her rags from last year."

The zaddik of Kálló and his companion looked up at a small opening above the oven. The pretty, blond head of a girl with sad, blue eyes peeped down from there.

The rebb's face lit up, "Listen, Reb Dov, and you too, Sarah. I am asking you for your daughter's hand. We'll have the wedding in three weeks with God's help. The groom is my foster son. His name is Yisroel, and I shall provide for them as long as I live."

"Don't make fun of us, Rebbe," lamented the woman who had already recognized the zaddik of Kálló." "She doesn't even have a dress to wear."

"Be quiet, woman!" the rebbe yelled at her. "Let's shake hands on it, *tekias kaf*[5] will be sufficient. We won't even draw up a document. That's right. And with this we've performed the *tenoim*.[6] I shall send your daughter four dresses: one made of velvet, the other of silk, the third of lace, and the fourth for the wedding made of gold yarn. I shall send you food and drink, as much as needed. Make preparations for three hundred guests in your courtyard. I shall perform the ceremony three weeks from today. And take a bath in honor of the festive occasion, Rev Dov. There's plenty of water in the well."

Jumping and dancing like a little boy, he got on the wagon. The blue spring air was full of song and laughter. The horses paced happily in the sand on their way out of the village. The rebbe began singing in the driver's seat. "We're going home, to Kálló," he told Reb Shayeh Aaron Fisch.

Reb Dov Wasserschepper just stood by the well. He looked after them, grumbled something in his beard, and shook his head.

A Hasidic Wedding in the Eighteenth Century

Play, gypsy! There is a great celebration in Levelek.

Well, there were no gypsies on hand, but instead there were six handpicked *klezmers*[7], who came over from Tass where they had been staying since Purim. Well, there could be a great celebration even without gypsies. In the courtyard, at the end of the village, a large table was set where the bride and groom sat looking at each other lovingly. The zaddik of Kálló sat at the head of the table. His graying hair—Reb Eizik was well in his forties—looked gilded in the bright July sun. And there were the wedding guests: the entire Jewish population of Levelek, Kálló, Pagony, Apagy, Napkor, and Semény.[8] At least three hundred Jews who even brought their wives along. There were guests from as far as Kemecse[9] and Tass. Never had there been seen a wedding like this in Szabolcs county. Even His Excellency, the Judge of Levelek, András Jószántó (that is the name preserved in Jewish legend) came by, carrying his silver-capped cane and, after paying his respects sat down at the main table.

The sun had not set its rays on a more beautiful young couple in the county. Yisroel, the foster child of the zaddik of Kálló, had grown into a fine young man of eighteen. The women could hardly take their eyes off his finely chiseled profile, rimmed by golden locks, his high, pensive forehead, and his eyes in which aristocratic kindness and carefreeness smiled. And the bride was like Cinderella, who came out of the ashes of the oven and turned into a princess. The Chaveh of Reb Dov Wasserschepper, the blond little Eva looked like an angel in her white wedding dress. Her mother, who had washed herself clean for the occasion, could not admire her enough. Her father, already a little tipsy, glanced toward the young pair mischievously. But Chaveh looked at neither of them. Her eyes were locked in Yisroel's eyes. They sat together oblivious of the happenings around them. They even forgot to partake of the golden soup that was usually served at weddings to the bride and groom who, according to custom, fasted on the day of the great event. They looked at no one except each other, as if they had finally found each other after long wandering.

Still, there would have been a great deal to see if they had looked around. Two *marshaliks*[10] competed in the making of good humor. Mechl from Sziget and Weintraub from Bzezany were great competitors. The two *marshaliks* had never worked together at a wedding before. Each had his own clientele. Weintraub had Ung, Bereg, Ugocsa, and Bihar.[11] Mechl had Máramaros, Szabolcs, and the rest of the northern counties. Happy was the man at whose house these *marshaliks* appeared, at Purim, at a wedding, or at the birth of a child. But now they met. After all, an honorable *marshalik* had to make a showing at a celebration given by the zaddik of Kálló, even if it meant coming from the ends of the earth. Two *marshaliks,* two such *marshaliks* together—anybody could see that there was going to be trouble.

For the time being, they got along well in front of the *chuppah.*[12] The *chosnbezingen*[13] was given to *marshalik* Mechl. No eye remained tearless when he began,

Her nur zi, mein lieber chosn
Di zollst mir leben in simche vesosn.[14]

and then came a teasing verse, full of sad and joyous recount-
ing, of the parents gone, of the kindness of the zaddik of
Kálló as the foster father, of the approaching honeymoon,
and of other interesting things. In the meantime, the
marshalik from Galicia, who was entrusted with the *kale-
bezingen*,[15] made the bride and womenfolk cry.

At the table, however, the friendship between the two
marshaliks ended. They began to make fun of each other,
to the great delight of those present. Mechl, the younger
of the two—this wandering Bohemian wore an impossible
green necktie with the traditionally large, black *marshalik*-
coat that touched the ground—knew Weintraub's weakness.
The latter liked to speak in allegories and was fond of parables
and tales. Mechl, on the other hand, preferred talmudic sayings; he liked to quote and vary them, to throw them around
with great skill like a circus juggler twirling his iron stick.
Before the dinner was served, Mechl stood on the table, and
like a rabbi on the pulpit, started to recite the verse of a
psalm with great seriousness,

"*Eftecho bemoshol pi, abio chidos mini kedem.*"[16]

Then, turning toward his rival, Weintraub, he proceeded
to explain the sentence, "*Eftecho bemoshol*—he who works
with allegories, like you Weintraub, *pi—piha*,[17] it isn't worth
a thing. *Abio chidos*—I, however, quote the sayings of the
wise; *mini kedem*—which are found in our holy books."

Great laughter followed his explanation, Apparently
Mechl had got the better of his rival. But Weintraub was
not a man to give in easily. He jumped on the table and
started explaining the same poor tortured verse in his own
style.

"*Eftecho bemoshol*—even if I work with allegories; *pi*—

they are my own thoughts; *Abio chidos*—but you, Mechl, always cite old sayings; *mini kedem*—which you stole from the ancient books."

The audience, which laughed for several minutes, proved that his snappy answer had reached its mark. Mechl was speechless. It also proved that dueling, which the two *marshaliks* performed with that verse of the psalm, had not disappeared from the memory of Jews.

And with that introduction, not only did the feast begin but the fireworks of Jewish humor as well. For the time being, however, the zaddik of Kálló did not take part in the revels of his companions. He sat quietly, smiling. He was dressed in a kaftan made of white silk and wore white sandals. A wide belt made of purple velvet was tied around his waist and he had a glittering brown fur cap on his head. He leaned back in his chair like a Polish prince, looking at the festive crowd and the young pair. His followers were about to dance. Some of them danced with their women holding two corners of a handkerchief without touching one another as was the custom in performing the *mitzvoh*-dance at weddings. The kaftans, mackinaws, and other kinds of hasidic dresses were whirling around. The pointed caps twirled in the air like the reels of the merry-go-round. The zaddik of Kálló, however, did not like it if men danced with women (and later he even issued an order concerning it and taught a dance himself to the men that they could do with one another) and thus the commotion subsided and the *klezmers'* violins became silent. The two *marshaliks* announced the wedding gifts: the *chosn tsad*[18] was virtually the entire Jewish population of Kálló. The Jews of the county's seat (it was Nagykálló then) also gave a good account of themselves in their generosity. The *kale tsad*[19] did not measure up to its counterpart. The family of the watering Jew was neither well liked nor greatly respected in Levelek. It was customary for the groom to say a short *derosheh;*[20] after all, the *derosheh-geschenk*[21] was given in recognition of it. But the thoughts

of Yisroel, the groom, were elsewhere. He was whispering
lovingly to Chaveh and wasted no time with the guests. So
their attenion reverted to the *marshaliks* and once again
the Jewish humor took over.

The *marshaliks* started the fun and the guests soon joined
in. The many jokes and witty remarks sparkled above the
festive crowd, and decades later people were still talking
about the numerous remarks that had been made there.

Even the rebbe warmed up. He allowed himself three
jokes on that notable day. He told about the time when he
was a *bocher*[22] and went begging in Sziget one day wearing
muddy boots. A well-to-do Jew ordered him out of his
house because he feared that the young man would smear
mud all over his room. The *bocher* dropped a remark, "Do
you know, Reb Doved, that you resemble God in many
ways?"

Reb Doved gave him a surprised look and shook him
by the ear, thinking that he was being ridiculed.

"I wasn't making fun of you," replied the *bocher*. "Of
God we say in our daily prayer *merachem al-hooretz*[23] and
merachem al-haberiyos,[24] in other words, with God the earth
comes first and then man. It is the same with you, Reb
Doved. First comes the earth, the floor of your house, and
then man."

"Why is the *kesubboh*[25] written in Aramaic?" That is
how the rebbe's second story began. "So that the angels who
know no Aramaic wouldn't understand it. When Moses
arrived in Heaven in order to receive the Torah for Israel
they resisted him fiercely. They didn't want mortals to
receive the holy treasure. God, however, appeased them by
saying that the Torah had to be studied devoutly day and
night and for that the angels had no time. 'The men of Israel,'
said the Lord, 'will devote their lives to the Torah and their
women will carry the burden of daily life. They will take
care of the house and provide for the livelihood of the
family.' The angels reluctantly acquiesced in that and thus
Moses received the Torah for Israel. But what happened?

We can see that nowadays among Jews it is the man, not the woman, who bears the burden of daily life and it is already specified in the *kesubboh* that the man must respect, provide for, and take care of his woman—which means that he will devote his time not to the Torah but to the making of provision for his family. If the angels knew this," concluded the rebbe, "what great commotion would be in Heaven and what revolt against God! But they have no idea of all this; after all they don't know Aramaic, only Hebrew. And that is why the *kesubboh* is written in Aramaic."

When the rebbe looked around amid the great merriment that followed the conclusion of his story, he noticed tears in the eyes of the women (which proved that in poor Jewish families it was the woman after all who bore the burden of daily life). He smiled and made one more kind remark, "How often do we see tears in the eyes of women but how seldom do we see a man crying? If a woman cries in front of a man, she knows what she is doing. But a man feels that it would be futile to weep in front of his wife. Why? Because God made man of dust and water, and the flow of tears would soften dust. But God created woman of bone—of man's bone—and bone is not affected by water, it can resist tears. That is why women cry if they want to get something, because they know that it will be easy to soften their men. And for the same reason a man will not even attempt to cry, because he knows that he would find but hard bone, which his tears will not soften."

The witty explanation made the tears dry up in the eyes of the women and brought smiles instead.

That is how time passed at the wedding of Levelek. It was time for the after-the-meal prayer. The zaddik of Kálló, a cup of wine in each hand, began to sing in a melodic tone the old Hebrew poem prescribed by ritual:

> *Devai hoser*
> *Vegam chorayn*
> *Veoz illem*
> *Beshir yorayn.*[26]

Still, something remained that was disturbing. In vain the dancing, music, and jokes. In vain the sweet, catchy tunes of the violin above the table. Like a light veil, the general merrymaking was just fluttering over the big, big question.

No one knew the secret of the wedding of Levelek.

The eyes and lips of everyone seemed to be asking the silent questions, "What is the meaning of all this? Who is Yisroel, the groom? Who is Chaveh, the bride? What is the meaning of the unusual proposal? What was the purpose of the rebbe's nightly journeys? The midnight apparition on the highway, which led the zaddik of Kálló to Levelek? What is that unusual, great secret fluttering over the wedding at Levelek?"

Everyone was waiting for answers.

It was already dark when the prayer ended and torches were lit above the main table. The guests divided into groups and some began leaving. Others, accompanied by the *klez-mers*, moved into an arbor and struck up the famous tune:

> The cock is crowing already
> It will be dawn soon
> If God willed me for you
> I shall be yours . . .

Surrounded by a small group of friends, the rebbe remained in the garden. Alcohol was poured into large tin plates and was lit. Small blue and purple flames danced on the surface of the burning liquid mirror. The people took some of the burning alcohol on their long spoons. The pipes released big stacks of smoke and everyone' was waiting for the rebbe's words in deep silence.

For he had to say something.

Above, the stars lit up. At times, the howling of village dogs interrupted the distant, quiet sound of the violins. The fresh fragrance of summer oozed in from the meadows.

The zaddik of Kálló looked around, "Listen, Rebboysem.

I am going to tell you the miraculous story of Yisroel and Chaveh, the groom and bride, the prince and the princess."

And the zaddik began telling his story.

The Soul of the Fugitive Prince

There was a prince who lived in Spain three hundred years ago. His name was Thaddeus.

The times of Prince Thaddeus were sad ones. The sky was often red above the Spanish lands. Stakes were burning on the fields and in the great market places. They burned Jews on them, Jews who did not want to abandon their faith and who died in the flames with the name of God on their lips.

Prince Thaddeus was the head of that institution which sought out Jews in the country and cast them into jail. He was the Chief Inquisitor of Spain.

He was not to be blamed. It was his upbringing that prepared him for that role. His father, a bloodthirsty king, and his mother, an evil queen, wanted their firstborn child to grow up knowing blood and death.

Prince Thaddeus was a quiet, taciturn, and obedient boy. He signed the execution papers that were put before him. He obeyed his father's order commanding him that he be present at the terrible burnings. But the dying could see that his face saddened at hearing their prayers, and his soul, like a frozen lake, gradually became serious and sorrowful. No one knew that there was something slumbering in him. At the age of twenty-five, the hair of Prince Thaddeus was already gray, and deep and tired lines stretched across his face.

His life was as cold and punctual as the big clock with its heavy, golden driving weights that stood on his table. He rose early, went to Mass, prayed, and then the guilty who were to be put to death on that day were presented before him in the Palace of the Inquisition. Prince Thaddeus looked them over and the lines on his face deepened. But he said nothing. With one movement of his hand, he sent them to their death. He ate with his parents in the royal palace at noon, and visited his fiancée, Princess Angela, afterwards.

Princess Angela was the cousin of Prince Thaddeus. At an early age they were already engaged, as arranged by their parents, and they were not even ten years old when the Bishop of Burgos blessed them as if they were already married.

Princess Angela was just as quiet and taciturn as her fiancé. She disliked people and her soul was weighed down by the dark Spanish sky dimmed by the smoke of the stakes. She loved her quiet prince devoutly, and both of them, like two sad, weary flowers, were slowly withering away day by day in that hatefully burning and suffocating atmosphere.

But in the afternoon, Prince Thaddeus devoted his time to science. Then his soul was enlivened, and with his master in the study, he buried himself in the huge folios. The human sciences opened up before him. The two men studied the globe, which a hidden clock spring made revolve on its golden stand. The wisdom of Latin codices echoed from the faded parchments. The knowledge, tales, and history of foreign peoples filled the vaulted hall. It was apparent that the prince's tutor knew a great deal.

His name was Leon de Coronel. At the court, everyone called him Dr. Leon for short. He had come to the royal court from the University of Barcelona. He was entrusted with the education of the prince. His pupil was already twenty-three years old. His sad soul responded well to Dr. Leon, who could always tell him something new in his deep, melodic voice. The plays of numbers, the tricky details of algebra, the mysterious movement of the stars, the formidable signs of the constellations, the fabled descriptions of geography, and the rational rules of grammar and spelling— Dr. Leon de Coronel knew them all.

Following the bloody mornings, the prince longed for the quiet afternoons when he sent his soul, like a butterfly fluttering above the waves of the sea, into the distance, into a better, happier world. And when it happened that in the afternoon those condemned to death were led away under his window and that the singing of psalms from the lips of the bound Jews reached his ears, Prince Thaddeus started up from his daydreams, ran to the window, and closed its huge, iron slabs in order to block out the sounds. At such times, Master Leon, the prince's tutor, turned aside. His face turned pale and his black beard trembled. It was obvious that he was also deeply affected by the song of those going to their death.

Prince Thaddues and the wise Dr. Leon were very fond of each other. They often discussed the mysteries of life sitting in the colonnade in the starlit nights. At such times, the words of Dr. Leon were like those of a great man of God—reassuring, sad, and respectful toward Heaven. And Prince Thaddeus felt that the priests he knew, like Thomas Torquemada and Peter Arbuez, the bloodthirsty bishops and cardinals, who, like hyenas, dug up the bones of dead Jews and jubilantly carried them to the stake, were no priests at all and did not know God. There was only one wise man in the whole of Spain, one true priest, and that was his tutor, Leon de Coronel.

Early one morning before he went to Mass, the Prince unexpectedly went to Dr. Leon's apartment, which was in the northern wing of the palace. It was not his custom to visit his tutor, but a scientific problem troubled him throughout the night and he was in a hurry to seek a solution to it. He was suprised to find Dr. Leon's rooms empty. The scholar could not be found anywhere. Where could he be so early in the morning?

The prince was about to leave when suddenly unusual sounds struck his ears—wailing, crying, lamenting sounds similar to the chanting of hymns. He began searching the rooms excitedly. In front of one of the large bookshelves the singing grew stronger. The prince leaned on it in order to hear better and suddenly the shelf, moved by a spring, opened up.

Prince Thaddeus made the sign of the cross in his horror. He walked through the secret passage and found himself in a small, narrow room where, as in a crypt, a night-light was burning dimly. There were innumerable large and old folios on the walls. In the middle of the room a small, unusual-looking bureau stood with its door open. The prince then saw his tutor, Leon de Coronel, who stood in front of a small table on which a scroll of parchment lay. Wrapped in a large blue-rimmed veil and a black strap tied around his arm and forehead, there stood the wise man bowing, crying, and praying.

The prince was flabbergasted. Trembling, he cried out, "Marrano! You are a Marrano, too, my poor master!"

Dr. Leon did not interrupt his prayer. The prince stood there motionless, listening to the same sorrowful song that he knew so well from the lips of those condemned heretics. When Dr. Leon finished his morning prayer he turned and said calmly to the prince, "Yes, I am a Marrano, too. One of the *anusim*—as our sacred language calls them—who were forced to convert to Christianity, but I could not deny my God and my people. I am a Marrano, a secret Jew, Prince, like the many thousands whom your spies have found among my poor brothers. And now send me to the stake, great Inquisitor!"

Dr. Leon stood there with shining eyes, happily and proudly. The prince sank into a chair speechlessly.

"I am ready, Prince," said Dr. Leon. "It is not painful to part with life. I shall be united with the souls of my brothers that have ascended in fire before the throne of the Lord. I was prepared for the chance that one of these days your spies would break in here and capture me. What daring it is after all to set up a little synagogue in the palace of the King of Spain! But as long as you are already here, Prince, look around. Look at our realm and see for the sake of what we go to the stakes. Look at the books of the Talmud that are burned with us. But they rise from the flames and survive your executioners. Look at a Torah parchment, which we tie around our waist in death like a dying soldier the flag of his country. Look at the horn, which we take secretly to abandoned meadows and barren mountains in an early fall morning when we proclaim the new year. Look at the unleavened bread, whose crumbs we preserve in secret as your priests preserve gold. And look at our wandering life, below the ground, in caves and behind secret passages. Like a lover from his beloved, we cannot be separated from our God!"

The prince's face began to glow. He embraced Dr. Leon and said to him quietly: "I shall not send you to the stake, Master Leon. But don't you send me back into the world of my ancestors, either. I want to share your secret because I know that you are the sole cure for my poor, evil-ridden soul. Your wisdom and your faith. I shall die if you leave me. Give me your faith, Master Leon. I want to believe, too. I want to love after so much hatred. I want to be a Jew, Master Leon."

For three months, Leon de Coronel taught the prince and his fiancée the Jewish faith in great secret. They sat and listened to the laws of Moses and the teachings of Hillel and Akiba in secret rooms above which the happy sounds of royal parties were heard. They learned to pray in Hebrew and Prince Thaddeus, pretending to be ill, entered the Palace of Inquisition no more. He transferred his sad duties to a cardinal.

After three months, the prince converted to the Jewish faith and received the name of Yisroel. His fiancée, Princess Angela, became a Jewess in the crystal water of an abandoned lake among the wives and daughters of persecuted Marranos. Her new name was Chaveh.

They knew that the spies of the Inquisition would be after them, and would seek out the one who had dared help them abandon the Church. Because of that, their master, Leon de Coronel, left Madrid on a cloudy night. He fled through the smoldering country—in Seville, Granada, Saragossa, Segovia, Cordova, and Malaga, the stakes burned, the bells tolled, the holy processions sang, and the victims struggled before meeting death—and reached the seacoast, where he boarded a Turkish sailor's boat for Naples. There were members of his family, the Coronels, who lived openly in that city as Jews. All of them were Marranos who had fled from Spain earlier. Their ancestor was Abraham Senior, former treasurer of the king of Spain.

Soon afterward, the prince and the princess appeared before the king and queen. Calmly and quietly, Prince Thaddeus announced that he and his fiancée had converted to the Jewish faith and asked the powerful king of Spain to put an end to the Inquisition.

The bishop, the queen's confessor, who was standing in the audience, half fainted in his outrage and dropped the crucifix from his hand. The anger of the royal pair knew no bounds. At first, however, the king and queen begged the young pair to reconsider. The queen said that it was God who made the annihilation of heretics their sacred duty. The king told them about the riches, gold, and land that the dynasty had acquired from the estates of the executed Jews and Marranos. But the royal begging and appeals were in vain, just as their anger and threats were. Smiling, Prince Thaddeus and Princess Angela faced the outraged parents. They felt the courage of Moses, whom the haughty Pharao could not frighten even for a moment. And Prince Thaddeus stepped to the window, opened it, and exclaimed as he pointed to a large square where preparations were being made for the *auto-da-fé*,[27] the burning of Jews, "Look outside, King of Spain, at El-Quemadero.[28] They are about to burn Jews again. But not only Jews. They are burning your country, too—your riches and the future of the people of Spain. You are burning yourselves, not my poor, poor brothers!"

The king reached for his sword at hearing these words of prediction. He wanted to kill his son. But the queen grabbed his arm and shouted to the young pair, "I should send you to the stake. You are miserable heretics like the rest. But I shall not do that. I shall punish you more severely. Clear out of this land. Leave without your possessions and may death reach you as beggars in a foreign land! From now on there will be no royal prince and royal princess in Spain; Prince Thaddeus and Princess Angela are dead."

And it is written in the Spanish chronicles that the heirs to the throne, a prince and a princess, died mysteriously.

A few months later two unusual strangers aroused a great commotion in the ghetto of Krakow. They were a poor, shabby pair, who lived in the darkest house of the Jews' street by the Vistula. The man looked tired and bent, the woman pale and sick. The man was often seen in the foggy winter mornings dragging himself to the synagogue, where he sat in the last row. He placed his head upon his arms and often wept.

"A *baal teshiveh*,"[29] said the Jews.

They were the poorest among the poor of the Jews' street, who were charitable people and to whom it appeared that they had come from afar. There was hardly any life in them. The women in the neighborhood brought them soup, a little meat, and bread, but the man was losing strength by the day and his wife could no longer get out of bed.

Gradually the news went around that the two were punishing themselves by sacred fasting. The old rabbi of Krakow visited them and returned excitedly. He left strict orders with the community to provide the strangers with everything good, and that they should be held in great

respect because they had made a great sacrifice to the faith
of Israel.

The Jews' street was buzzing with the exciting news. Its
people began to surround the stranger as if he were a zaddik,
and a doctor, the court physician of a Polish prince, was
called to the bed of the sick woman. He observed sadly
that it was only a matter of a few days. The effects of prolonged wandering and starvation had broken the poor
woman's heart.

One day the stranger fainted and remained unconscious
for a long time. When he revived at last, he said to those
standing around him: "My soul traveled up there. And up
in Heaven I was told that I would have to leave you. I shall
die tomorrow."

The woman, who was lying on the bed next to his, said:
"I shall go with you."

They died in the same hour. As befitting the pious, they
recited the psalms of the dying, and the *viduy*, the prayer
of repentance. They prayed the ancient request: *"Shimu no
rabbosay, hare ani moser modoo lifnechem* . . . I shall make
a confession before you, my masters. Help me so I may
stand in purity and beauty in front of the throne of the Lord.
Praise be to the Lord forever, Amen. I am seeking for-
giveness from all those whom I offended." The rabbi of
Krakow then closed the tired eyelids.

The two strangers of the ghetto of Krakow were laid to
rest in the old cemetery by the Vistula. The rabbi had simple
tombstones erected for them. One was inscribed "Yisroel,"
the other "Chaveh." He also had two small royal crowns
engraved in each of the stones. Only he knew their secret;
the people never learned it.

The two graves with their tombstones inscribed in
Hebrew and decorated with the royal crowns were swept
away by the torrents of a high tide.

When the souls of the prince and princess reached Heaven, the angels were already waiting for them at the outer wall of Eden. They took off the white dresses of the dead and gave them transparent gold robes. Beautiful crowns were placed on their heads and branches of myrtle in their hands. The angel Azriel embraced the soul of the prince and Peniel the soul of the princess, and they set out toward the throne of the Lord.

They crossed the inner wall of Eden, which was made of black fire, then the second, made of red fire, and finally the last one, made of white fire. They walked through a garden, where they noticed the pious sitting under small canopies in glittering brightness. Wondrous flowers spread a spicy fragrance and there were golden grapevines by the divans of the pious on which the grapes were real pearls. The pious were singing psalms to the Lord.

They also saw the great men of Israel, kings and writers, sitting on silver chairs. On a separate, small platform, under palms and cedars, the prophet Elijah sat, and at his feet the Messiah. He placed his head in the prophet's lap weeping. He lamented loudly, "I am crying for my people Israel. How they are suffering! How they believe in me! And I cannot go to redeem them because my time has not yet come."

And they saw Gadiel, the Jewish child whom the Roman soldiers killed at the age of seven as he was studying the Torah. His little body was intact again. He was sitting in the grass with the Bible in his lap for which he had suffered the penalty of death. He was explaining it to the pious.

When they arrived at the end of the Garden of Eden after a long walk, they found themselves in front of the heavenly court. The *hore esh,* the mountains of fire, were to the right; the *hore sheleg,* the mountains of snow, were to the left, and each mountain was but a step leading to the throne of the Lord. A million angels stood at the base of the throne. To the right, music was playing, flutes and horns, the pious were praying in the Garden of Eden and the words

of the great heavenly *Kaddish*,[30] in praise of God, were heard.
To the left, in the depth, the sinners suffered and the word
Amen was heard, which the suffering wicked said in response
after each sentence. That Amen was the prayer by which
they declared their recognition of God's eternal power and
glory.

The two trembling souls stood in front of the throne
of the Lord. The angel Mahariel was their defender, and
Barkiel, their prosecutor. Mahariel told of their repentance,
piety, poverty, and good deeds. He beseeched the Lord to
allow them to remain among the pious in the Garden of
Eden. But Barkiel's accusation thundered: how many thousands of poor souls had perished because of Prince Thaddeus and how many innocent people he had sent to their
deaths! Such guilty persons cannot remain among the pious.
First, they must be purified in the Gehinnom, in the hell
of fire and suffering. They would not have to stay there forever; after they suffered they would return to their place
in the Garden of Eden.

The prince's soul trembled under the terrible accusation
and cried out in front of the Lord's throne, "I feel that I
have sinned and I know that I must repent in order to
deserve the tranquillity and happiness of Eden. But do not
punish me by suffering in fire. Send me back to earth instead.
Let my soul live through another life, a pious, pure life and
after that let me return here, like a person who has bathed
in spring water, and then give us a place at the throne of
the Lord."

Laughter and merriment broke out among the hundreds
of thousands of angels. The singing of psalms could be heard
in the endless space. The angel Metatron came fluttering
down the steps and announced God's decision. The two
souls were to return to earth so that they might be purified
in new, pious lives and share the ethereal happiness of the
pious.

Suddenly, powerfully, like thunder, and quietly like a

breeze, a voice came down from the heights. It was the voice of God. He said, "Will they find each other on earth if they come to a new life? Will they not separate from each other in their earthly lives? Will they not search for each other in vain, suffering? Go, Gabriel, accompany them and tell my servants on earth who know Me that those two souls must meet again, that they must live together and return here together. Because they love each other."

Gabriel wrapped the two trembling souls in his white robe, bowed before the infinite mercy of God, and prepared to descend. He plunged toward earth with the souls of Yisroel and Chaveh to meet their new lives. He became smaller and smaller and finally, like a comet, disappeared into the infinite night.

When the zaddik of Kálló reached that point in his story, he lapsed into silence.

"*Gilgul neshomos,* the wandering of souls. Our young pair . . . Are they, Rebbe?" someone inquired.

The zaddik nodded, "Yes, they are the ones, Rebboysem. After nearly three hundred years, the soul of the prince was reborn in a small village in Galicia. He returned as the son of a poor washerwoman. The Baal-Shem, my master, may his memory be blessed, received word about it from Heaven. After all, the angel Gabriel made sure that the servants of God (and the Baal-Shem was foremost of them) knew about the two souls. And the Baal-Shem took the small boy in whom the soul of the wandering prince lived. He taught and looked after him but he could not find the girl. He learned, however, in a secret vision, that the soul of the princess was reborn near me. And on his deathbed, he entrusted the boy to me. I gave him my sacred promise that I would seek out the girl in order that the two souls, according to God's order, might find each other. He also told me that he could not die peacefully until I came to him, but upon my arrival he could appear in front of the throne of the Lord and report that he had faithfully carried out the wish of the Creator."

"One is the son of a washerwoman," observed Reb Shayeh Aaron Fisch, "and the other is the daughter of a watering Jew. And they are a prince and a princess. Who would have believed it?"

The zaddik nodded, "This is the secret journey of the souls on earth. Who knows whose soul we carry on earth and for whom we yearn, and who it is we shall never reach? But the Lord took good care of these two souls. It was our responsibility to find them, Yisroel and Chaveh—they don't even know who they are. The soul has no recollection. But God remembers and now they will live in piety and poverty and the life to come will be theirs."

There was a brief pause, "But until I found the princess . . . Do you know for how many years I searched in vain? I did not receive word from Heaven. But God's mercy was infinite. He forgive my sins and considered me deserving of His message. He showed me the way through His messenger and fulfilled His will. And now I am ready to appear in front of His throne in peace. But Rebboysem," he added, "not a word to anyone about this. Let it remain our secret. Let the world, the parents, the relatives, even the new pair think that it was a simple wedding at Levelek. We know that it was more: a meeting. A meeting of souls. The soul of the wandering prince met here the soul of the princess."

It was already dawn. They were sitting around the zaddik in deep silence. And then they slowly started preparing for the morning prayer.

The wedding of Yisroel and Chaveh took place on June 17, 1770, on the 20th of Sivan,[31] in Levelek. No further information is known of them or of their family. It is said that they moved to Poland and spent their lives in piety. That is all anyone knows about them.

9

The Three Card Players

Someone Is Knocking on the Window

This miraculous tale begins on the eve of the Sabbath of *Yisro*.[1]

It is a great Sabbath, a memorable Sabbath. It is on this Sabbath that the Ten Commandments are read from the Torah, the gift of God, the pride of Israel. All of the worshipers are standing and their souls are filled with music as the cantor starts to recite the First Commandment. How his words sing and ring! They fly up off the parchment, and like sunshine flash through the dusty air of the synagogue. The spell of Sinai covers the tattered seats, an invisible veil is descending from the sky, and God's glory appears above the heads of the faithful. There are more solemn Sabbaths, sadder Sabbaths, and happier Sabbaths in the year, but no Sabbath is more beautiful than the one on which the Ten Commandments are given again to Israel's suffering children. It usually happens in the cold aftermath of winter; but when that Sabbath arrives the trees begin to shoot forth their buds, the barren land of the synagogue turns green, and the air is filled with the song of birds. Spring has come.

An unsual thing happened on the eve of the Sabbath of *Yisro*. A stranger entered the synagogue of Kálló. That in itself would not have been an unusual occurrence. However, when the cantor reached a certain verse in one of the Sabbath psalms, the stranger rose from his seat, walked the length of the entire synagogue up to the platform, and from there to the rabbi's seat. The zaddik of Kálló was swaying, deeply immersed in his prayers, and singing a sweet song. The stranger stepped to the zaddik and put his hand on his shoulder. The zaddik turned around and looked at him.

By that time the whole congregation took a better look at the reckless, bold man who dared to disturb the zaddik in prayer. He was a tall, bony, elderly Jew with gray beard and bushy eyebrows. He wore an old coat and there were large patches on his hat. What kind of a person would disturb the zaddik of Kálló so rudely?

The atmosphere of devotion was shattered. The cantor looked at the stranger with astonishment. The latter was engaged in a lively, almost threatening discussion with the zaddik, who merely looked at him and listened. But then he shrugged his shoulders and turned away to continue his prayers. It was as if he had said, "So what! Things like that have already happened."

The stranger turned around angrily, hurried off the podium, and ran out of the synagogue.

When Reb Dovid, the cantor, finished with the *Kiddush*[2] and the people started to leave, it was the presumptuous stranger who became the general topic of conversation. Could he not have waited for the end of the service to speak with the zaddik? Reb Chayyim Tarcal, who had been in Kálló for only two weeks, was the angriest. Had anything like that been seen before? A nobody who pressed his way to the zaddik's chair! There must be order in this congregation.

A crowd was forming around the zaddik. Who was the stranger? What did he want? Where did he come from? What did he bring? The zaddik just smiled. They stood in the courtyard bombarding him with questions, but the zaddik did not respond.

Suddenly someone elbowed his way through the ranks

of people, pushing them aside. When he reached the zaddik, he grabbed his coat and began to pull him out of the circle of inquirers. Had anything like that been seen before?

As well as could be made out in the darkness, it was a tall, red-bearded Jew—no one knew him—who pulled the zaddik away. They stood on the stairs at the threshold of the synagogue. The stranger spoke, explaining and demanding. Then the zaddik turned away from him and returned to his followers. And he smiled as he said, "I don't care about it. I want to rest on the Sabbath."

Nobody knew who the stranger was or what he wanted. The zaddik would not say a word about the unusual happening. He just kept smiling and shrugged his shoulders. There was nothing to be done but to go home and wait for the outcome of events.

The zaddik returned to his house. Only a few of his followers were invited that evening for a dinner of tasty fried fish. They stood at a respectful distance, waiting for the zaddik to enter his room.

According to tradition, angels accompany the pious from the synagogue to their homes on Friday evening. The zaddik stood alone in front of the door of his room, then, as if talking to his Sabbath angels, walked to the festive table. He blessed the members of his family and those living in his house. Then he sang *Sholem aleychem,* the greeting of angels: "White angels, the angels of peace, God's messengers, beloved angels of the Sabbath: welcome! Bless us, bring blessing upon us, take blessing from us, and protect us from misfortune and pestilence. Angels . . . angels . . . angels of the Sabbath." And the zaddik walked around the table, followed by the members of his family, singing the songs of the Sabbath. They were mysterious, secret, and subdued melodies. In them the music of the hereafter quivered, Israel's thousandfold suffering, the happiness of the home, and the infinite joy of family life. It was the eve of the Sabbath.

The zaddik was cheerful and satisfied. He sang and

smiled throughout the whole evening. After the dinner, at the time of the *Zemiros*,[3] he started the singing himself. What music! What songs! A Hungarian melody was followed by a Jewish one, each of which had its own story. One was brought from Patak[4] last winter, where an itinerant Russian cantor sang it. Another from Nikolsburg,[5] straight from the zaddik's table there. Others the zaddik of Kálló had learned from wandering shepherd children, whereas some, it is told, the Levites had sung in Jerusalem at one time. One was slow and sad; the other cheerful and lively like the candlelight in the large, silver candelabrum. The zaddik sang in a loud voice; Reb Shayeh Aaron Fisch, the zaddik's majordomo, followed his master's exuberant singing in a much lower, respectful tone; Reb Chayyim Tarcal only nodded his head rhythmically. After all, how would he dare to disturb the heavenly beauty of the zaddik's song? The fourth, Reb Modche Patak, just sat there listening to the songs with his eyes closed. But despite the beautiful songs and the enchanting music, the zaddik's followers were preoccupied with trying to find answers to the persistent questions: Who were those two mysterious men? What did they want? Where did they come from?

The zaddik started to sing the most beautiful of Sabbath melodies for the third time. When he reached the verse "—he who protects the Sabbath from being violated will be greatly rewarded"—he suddenly stopped and began to explain its meaning. "Do you know, Rebboysem, how I understand the meaning of this verse? I understand it to mean that not only he who observes the Sabbath is the doer of meritorious service, but also the one who keeps others from violating the Sabbath. That is the real meaning of those words. What do you think?"

The three faithful obviously thought of something but had no time to explain it, for suddenly someone knocked on the window. The zaddik shook at the unexpected noise and turned toward his disciples, "That is the third time that I am called for this evening." He got up frowning, walked to the window, and opened it.

A stream of cool air rushed in from the garden. The light of the candles flared up. Reb Chayyim glanced toward the window but—he confessed it later—saw only elegantly dressed men and women stepping down from a carriage surrounded by blinding brightness. They walked to the window and spoke with the zaddik. Reb Shayeh Aaron did not even dare to open his eyes, and he swore later that he had heard the rolling of wheels in that mysterious moment, followed by words spoken in Hebrew. Reb Modche, who covered his eyes and even plugged his ears out of piety, recalled the rustling of silk and velvet and a bright lilac-colored light glittering on the window. None of them had time, however, to reflect upon his experience in greater detail because the zaddik closed the window and sat down again at the table.

"Let us pray, my friends," he said.

They prayed, solemnly and quietly. Then the zaddik got up and said to his disciples, "Leave word for the cantor to start the morning service a little later. Tell your women that you will not be at home tonight. Then come back. Tonight we shall remain together."

The three Jews bowed and the rebbe smiled, "Yes, until morning. I have an urgent task to perform and I have been reminded of it three times already. You are going to come with me to Nyiregyháza[6] tonight."

To Nyiregyháza on Friday night? More than a good ten miles' distance. Perhaps even farther. By wagon, even if drawn by fast horses, it would take three hours from Kálló. But to ride on a wagon on Friday night?

The zaddik of Kálló could not be serious. What about on foot?

On foot it would take a day's walk. But the Law forbids such a long journey on the Sabbath. It is permissible to take two thousand steps, perhaps two thousand more with a little

bit of cunning, with skillful dodging among the iron teeth of
the Law. But a day's journey! What had gotten into the
zaddik of Kálló?

Nothing seemed to disturb the zaddik of Kálló. He just
sat there calmly and kept smiling. Then he looked at his
three dumbfounded disciples and said, "Why are you still
here? Have you not heard my orders? Go home and hurry
back so we may leave for Nyiregyháza."

Reb Shayeh Aaron Fisch, Reb Chayyim Tarcal, and Reb
Modche Patak got up slowly. It made no sense to ask any
more questions. The zaddik spoke and they had to obey.
In a half hour they were back in the zaddik's reception room,
dispirited but ready to go. The zaddik was still sitting at the
table. There were a few pieces of *challah*[7] in front of him.
His eyes stared into the burning candles, and the sweet
Friday evening melody was still on his lips. He appeared
to be looking into the distance of a thousand miles.

"Are you back, Rebboysem? Then we can go."

The zaddik and his three bodyguards walked quietly
along the dark main street. All four wore festive hats. The
zaddik had on a pair of new boots that he had received
from the city of Miskolc[8] the day before. The other three
wore black festive suits, fur hats, and fur-collared coats. They
were cold in the fresh March air.

The people of Kálló were already asleep. There were only
a few dim lights flickering in the night. The wife of Iczig
the tailor was leaning out of a window that was cut into
the garden door when she noticed the four black wanderers.
She screamed and ran into the house. In the Cifras's house
the candles were still burning and the sounds of singing were
heard. The zaddik stopped at the house and knocked on the
door. Good Sabbath!

There were fewer and fewer houses as they walked on,
and the air got colder. The sad yelping of a dog was heard
from the depth of the gardens. The grass became moister
and their feet began to stick to the soil; the wanderers

reached the highway. A few more deserted shacks and the city ended.

Reb Shayeh Aaron was confused. What was going to happen? What was going happen? He had gone through many a venture on the zaddik's side, but he had never taken part in anything like this one. There was surely something mysterious about it. The zaddik of Kálló had received three messages: one in the synagogue, one in the courtyard of the synagogue, and one as they were sitting at dinner. He was called three times; but where and by whom? Whose emissaries were those strangers in the synagogue? From whom did those mysterious guests at dinnertime bring orders? It was to these questions that Reb Shayeh Aaron sought answers. His beard was hanging down and he was rubbing his hands together. He was thinking so intensely that he almost tripped and fell on some protruding stones.

Suddenly they stopped. It was the end of the city. There were no windows, no lights anywhere. Only the stars were shining in the eternal height and the grass at their feet kept bending back and forth in the cool wind of the night as they passed the last shack. Reb Chayyim reached out and touched a piece of wire stretched out between two trees. It was the outer limit of the city.

Until then none of them spoke. Suddenly the zaddik of Kálló asked, "Is that the *erev*, Reb Chayyim?"

It was the *erev*, the Sabbath border wire for all pious Jews, the sign marking the end of the town. It was only as far as the *erev* that on the Sabbath Jews were allowed to carry a thing or two. One could even walk beyond the *erev*. But only two thousand steps. Not a step beyond that, except in unusual cases. There was an established limit marking the end of these two thousand steps, too. It was at the turn of the highway, near the steppe of Harangod, where a tall, lightning-stricken poplar stood on guard. There was a small pile of bricks, and under the pile a small pit, and next to the pit, the poplar. No one could walk beyond that. From

that spot on, it was up to the zaddik of Kálló what he wanted
to accomplish with his travel plans on the night of the
Sabbath.

And as the four of them were standing by the wire in
the darkness, the zaddik said, "And now, Rebboysem, we
are going to take a little walk in the night. I am going . . ."
He paused for a moment and then continued, "and Reb
Shayeh Aaron is coming with me . . . ," and he stopped again.
"And Reb Modche and Reb Chayyim are coming with
me. . . ." There was another moment of silence. Then the
zaddik cried out in a strong voice, "And *you* are coming with
me! Yes, *you!* Don't resist! *You* are coming with me to
Nyiregyháza for the sanctification of His name!"

Trembling, the three Jews looked around. To whom was
he talking? There was no one else near. Reb Shayeh Aaron
Fisch began searching in the darkness. Suddenly, he caught
sight of the mysterious *you* to whom the zaddik was talking.
He stood there flabbergasted. It was the wire!

As the zaddik of Kálló was standing by the wire he
touched it then struck it twice. Then he burst out laughing,
"We can go now, my friends. Don't be afraid, it won't take
long."

Was it a dream or some unusual illusion? The participants
of the miraculous journey could never say. Reb Shayeh
Aaron clearly saw that the *wire moved,* and, together with
the two trees between which it was stretched out, started to
speed on the highway. Like some rumbling gate in the
night, the Sabbath gate kept ahead of them and they behind
it without having to step over it. What a going, what a
journey! As if they were on a magic carpet pulled by
mysterious hands, yet they stood at the same place on the
highway. In the sky, the stars circled in perpetual calm
and silence, whereas on the ground around them everything
was in motion, rushing in the night. Trees and bushes swept
along by them, disappearing in the fog, wrapped up in a veil
and melting into a colossal wall. Farms came into view and

disappeared by them at great speed, like small white spots with dim fires and mysterious draw wells. What was happening to them? Were they dizzy, dreaming, or were their eyes playing tricks on them? Reb Modche closed his eyes and his whole body trembled. Reb Chayyim quietly named the villages that they left behind, "Kiskálló . . . Nagyszállas . . . Nyíres . . . Szépkút."⁹

Only Reb Shayeh Aaron retained his composure and watched as carefully as he could. The zaddik was standing or walking—no one could say for sure—beside him, and he smiled. The wire, the Sabbath border, stretched in front of them. Reb Shayeh Aaron already understood what was happening to them. They did not leave or breach the Sabbath: *the Sabbath went with them* and they journeyed without having to step over its border. And Reb Shayeh Aaron also began to smile and his heart was filled with infinite happiness that he could be a participant in the miraculous night. He understood the zaddik and God's infinite grace; he thought of Abba Tachna, a talmudic sage for whom God had also performed a miracle with His Sabbath. Abba Tachna was in a great hurry late on a Friday afternoon, and it happened that he could not reach a city before the arrival of the Sabbath. God, may His name be blessed, pulled the sun back above the sky after it had already set, because He did not want him to break the Sabbath.

Suddenly, Reb Shayeh Aaron felt the zaddik's glance resting on him. The zaddik turned to his best and most faithful disciple and said: "Why don't you sing something? Don't fear and don't be alarmed."

What should a man sing in such a miraculous night? Like a well suddenly bubbling up in the depth of a forest, Reb Shayeb Aaron's soul was filled with an ancient song—an ancient song of an ancient miracle, of the fountainhead of truth, of the benefactor of Jewish mothers, of the great rabbi who is known to all Jews as Rabbi Meir the wonder-worker. Meir Baal-ha-Nes. And of that great miracle that happened to him when he set out to sea in order to save a prisoner from death on the opposite shore. Meir, the wonder-working rabbi, set out in the middle of the night on the infinitely great sea and crossed it. His feet remained dry as he kept walking on a silk scarf that the unfortunate prisoner's mother had given him to save her only son. How was it when Meir Baal-ha-Nes set out and crossed the great sea in one day?

"Amol iz der Rebbe ibern yam gefor . . ."[10]

The song formed timidly and quietly in Reb Shayeh Aaron's throat. When they heard the first tune, Reb Modche and Reb Chayyim recovered their wits and then the song really got under way in the night of the miracles, in their great speed:

> *Amol iz der Rebbe ibern yam gefor . . .*
> *Der Rebbe, Reb Meir Baal-ha-Nes*
> *Woz andere forn hindert yorn,*
> *Hat er gemacht in ein Mees lees*
> *In az der Rebbe fort, min hastam*
> *Furn doch alle chasidem mit.*[11]

And the refrain, the sweet, old, off-key refrain burst forth from the three throats:

> *In de alle apekorsem, de hiltayes*
> *Gleyben in dem allen nit!*[12]

"Those unbelievers," mused Reb Shayeh Aaron, "the bad Jews, and the doubters, will not believe a word of this miracle! They do not believe it of the sea, they do not believe it of Rabbi Meir. They do not believe? It is easy not to believe. For example, who would believe it of this night, of this present miraculous journey? And which one of the doubting, weak Jews will one day believe that the zaddik of Kálló walked to Nyiregyháza on a Friday night? And walk the way he did! We are almost here. At the curve the towers of Nyiregyháza are visible already. We have arrived."

Their great speed gradually decreased. The highway became wider. A few farms, painted white, were gleaming in the night as they slowly slid past them. Then the zaddik called out to the wire, "Stop!"

The journey came to an end. The wire lay in front of them motionless.

The zaddik issued the wire another command, "Stop and stay here until we have returned after having fulfilled our Creator's will."

Neither the wire nor the two trees moved. The wanderers passed under them.

"Reb Chayyim," said the zaddik of Kálló, "we have crossed the Sabbath border. According to our sacred laws we may take two thousand steps without breaking the Sabbath. Start counting, Reb Chayyim."

Reb Chayyim started counting. Two hundred steps, Világostanya; five hundred, the vineyards of Borbánya. Then a puddle, and in it they could see the reflection of Szarvas island. That was already a thousand steps. Then they reached Lake Bujtos. Five hundred steps more. Two hundred. One hundred.

They stood at the edge of the city in silence. Reb Chayyim kept counting.

Fifty steps more.

The last house of the city was a dilapidated tavern. First a stable, then the tavern.

Twenty steps more. The light of lamps inside reflected through the window. They walked in through the door, which was only loosely put in.

Reb Chayyim stopped counting. They had arrived.

There were candles burning on the table of the tavern. Beside the candles lay a big pile of gold and silver coins. And in the quivering semidarkness they noticed three large-bearded old Jews playing cards in the dimmed taproom.

They were playing cards on the sacred night of the Sabbath!

That roadside tavern that the zaddik of Kálló and his companions entered on that Friday night was known among the local people as the Bujtos Inn. The "Bujtos" spread out near the tavern. The "Bujtos" was a swamp, a marsh that never dried up, a large, sleepy puddle into which the bullrush and the reed nidnodded. It was still water stirred up only by the screaming of wild geese and ducks. The "Bujtos" was asleep at night; only the marshfire was seen wandering and bobbing up and down on the clump, and a sorrowful droning was heard in the direction of the reeds.

The Bujtos Inn was a notorious place. It was a gathering-place for wandering gypsies and highwaymen. Jews kept clear of it because its proprietor, János Oroszi Nagy, disliked their kind. And it was in that place that those three handsomely bearded Jews chose to play cards on the eve of that most sacred day.

The zaddik of Kálló stopped at the table, and the three players looked up.

"Where are you from?" asked the zaddik.

"From Tokaj," grunted one of them. "And who are you?"

"I am from Kálló."

"What do you want of us?" asked another. "The house is filled up. The innkeeper is already asleep. This is no place for a Jew."

"I have been called for to come to you," smiled the zaddik. "I have been told to come here and see what you were doing here on the night of the Sabbath."

Having said that, the zaddik of Kálló sat down at the other end of the table and motioned his disciples to do likewise. The players angrily threw away Satan's Bible.

"You have been called for?" screamed one of them. "And just who called for you? We don't need a kibitzer. We paid the innkeeper enough to let us stay here tonight. There is no need for guests, do you hear?"

The zaddik acted as if he did not hear the angry outburst. He remained seated, pulled his felt hat over his eyes, rested his head on his hand, and gave the players an impish look.

"I have been called for three times concerning you," he said cheerfully. "The first messenger said that you played cards across the entire land, playing at a different place every night. I told him that it was not my business. The second messenger reported that you were on your way here from Tokaj and that a band of robbers was following in your path, lurking about that pile of gold in front of you. I told him to let them lurk."

Suddenly there was silence in the tavern. One of the long-bearded players took a frightened glance at the money. Then he looked out of the window, searching for the band of robbers.

The zaddik calmly continued. "Then came the third messenger. It befits every Jew to visit the dying, so I came here to you, for you are like the dying."

The oldest of the players jumped to his feet, angry and frightened. "That is foolish talk," he yelled. "Who are you and what do you want of us?"

"I am a storyteller," replied the zaddik calmly, "a wandering *maggid*. I am going to tell you a story and then I shall be on my way. That is what I usually do with the dying; I have no time to waste with such lost people." He cleared his throat as was his custom before sermons.

"We don't want to hear your story," grumbled the old player. "Leave us alone. Here is a piece of gold and now off with you." And he pushed a gold piece in front of the zaddik.

"I don't need your gold," smiled the zaddik, "but there is someone behind you who wants it."

The men glanced beyond the table.

"I shall give him the gold coin," continued the zaddik, "he deserves it for his trouble. He has been with you day and night, and has not left you for a moment. He is standing behind you now. How his eyes are burning! How happy he

is! How he dances and applauds whenever you play cards!
Here you are, a small deposit for these precious souls! Here,
Satan, catch that coin!"

And with the hem of his cape, without his hand touching
it, the zaddik pushed the gold piece to the edge of the table.
It slid off the table, burst into a sharp, blue flame, and
disappeared. All this took place next to Reb Shayeh Aaron's
chair; he leaned over searching for the coin. It was not to be
found anywhere.

There was deathly silence in the room. The three players
stood side by side paralyzed with fear as they stared at the
zaddik. Who could this man be? Suddenly an expression of
recognition lit up the face of one. "The Kalever!" he whispered to the others.

The zaddik of Kálló! It could not be anyone else! The
great rabbi of Szabolcs county! God's servant and the
scourge of sinners! It was the zaddik of Kálló sitting in front
of them in the roadside tavern.

It was the zaddik of Kálló himself who came to
warn them on the night of the Sabbath. The three players
stood dumbfounded, waiting for what was going to happen.

"And now I am going to tell the story," said the zaddik
in a calm and peaceful voice.

In the darkened tavern, by the quivering light of candles,
with his three disciples on his right, the zaddik fixed his eyes
on the three players and began telling his story.

The Story

Above the stars where the Big Dipper ends and the
eternal brightness of Orion dims, the Kingdom of Heaven
starts.

There are seven kingdoms of Heaven, one above the
the other, like seven castles, like seven groves, like seven
seas, great and immense.

The name of the first is *vilon,* and its splendor is silvery, like the moon.

The name of the second is *rokiah,* and its light is purple, like the rising sun and like a ruby.

The name of the third is *shechokim,* and its color is like the opal and like fog.

The name of the fourth is *zevul,* and its brilliance is like the sleeping sea.

And the name of the fifth is *moon.* It blazes like pure gold. It is like a large, cheerful meadow—full of song, full of happiness, full of music.

And it is in that kingdom of Heaven that I shall start my story—in that fifth kingdom, where the music of the stars never ends, where there is neither day nor night.

Instead of the sun, letters provide light, letters whose brilliance is that of diamonds. They are the letters of the Torah, which fill the sky whirling, spinning, and flocking together to form shining, mysterious words. And instead of the moon, God's love shines gently, providing eternal light—that love by which He loves His people, Israel, in all worlds.

In this world there is never twilight, and in this Garden of Eden a magic meadow lies among silvery rivers. On the meadow, houses, huts, and cabins stand side by side forming an endless line.

Houses as far as the eye can see. A thousand, ten thousand, a million houses side by side. Strangely enough, however, some are only half-finished, others are not even started yet, and still others have progressed little beyond their foundations. Here and there the door has been installed but the roof is missing. Elsewhere, the doorway is missing. A pile of bricks lies next to each house. But there are no workers to build, and there are no stone-breakers to carry the bricks. These houses are built by no ordinary workers.

Each one has an owner, down on earth.

He is a mortal who lives, struggles, commits sins in his earthly life. And most of his kind think only of what will

happen to them in their lives on earth; only a few are concerned with their lives after death.

But one must think about that, too.

You should know that man not only needs shelter where
he can lay his head to rest on earth, but he also needs
shelter for his poor, wandering soul to rest somewhere in
the hereafter as well. It is not enough to find shelter down
here on earth; we must make sure that shelter is found up
there, in the infinity of times, under God's wings.

If we do good on earth—only a little bit of good—then
up there, in the fifth kingdom of Heaven, in that big meadow,
on that small lot which will be ours following our death, a
brick will move as the result of a good deed. Another good
deed and another brick is set in motion and adjusts itself
next to the one already placed. And so the process of construction is under way. If we refrain from sinning, a new
house is built up there. If we participate in the burial of
an abandoned dead; if we visit the lonely sick; if we make
things up to those who suffer innocently; if we help the
widow and the orphan; if we teach the Torah; if we sacrifice
ourselves for the name of the Lord—every like deed will
stir a brick into motion and build a house higher. And in
that house, which is called *binyan shel maaloh,* a heavenly
house, we shall find our haven after our death.

There are no builders, no workers up there; those houses
are built of earthly deeds. Only some mysterious, quiet movement is visible along the infinite line of houses; here and there
a brick rises suddenly and nestles close to another; a roof
becomes more complete, and the windows shine brighter.
When any one of these things happens, everyone knows that
someone has done something good down on earth.

The mysterious meadow in Heaven, however, is not
empty altogether. Mysterious figures walk up and down
among the rows of houses. Evil, contemptuous laughter is
heard on the streets.

Devils. The sons of Satan. The offspring of Shamael,

the fallen angel. Demons. Small and large. Young and old. And in the middle of the snickering, dancing army, the *Yetzerhore* himself, Satan.

He is examining the houses.

He bursts out laughing wherever the building of a house is progressing slowly. That soul will surely be his. He will spend his life down there in sin, uselessness, and frivolity. He does not think of his heavenly tranquillity or of building a shelter for himself up there. But when the moment of reckoning comes, the homeless soul will appear here and will have no place to rest. Then the soul will be his, Satan's, and he will take it with him into the yellow fire of Gehenna. But a good and honest soul is now about to complete its course on earth; the bricks are arranged one upon the other in thick rows: good deeds are being done in large number. Something has to be done. Satan lets out a whistle and commands one of his speedy demons to descend on earth so that he may entice the good soul to commit something sinful lest he die without having sinned.

And the inspection continues. From row to row, street to street, house to house. Satan is accompanied by his retinue. Suddenly, he stops. He jerks his shoulder so that his black cape will flutter in the air. There is something wrong here. *A house is almost finished here!*

Indeed, there stood a small heavenly house, already under its roof. Everything was put together in an orderly fashion; at the foundation 613 bricks, side by side in perfect order, which indicated that the builder of the house had fulfilled all of the 613 Mosaic commandments on earth. Its roof was finished: little square-shaped granite blocks—lifted up there by good deeds and blessings— shining brightly. Its staircase was also finished; beside the entrance, a small chair made of silver on which the pious builder would rest in the pleasant shadow of a palm tree and by the waves of a golden brook. What a life that must have been to have finished the small house with such perfection!

Satan was grumbling; he was dejected. Apparently he had lost a soul. Suddenly his countenance brightened. At the entrance, by the staircase, there was still an empty space, large enough for a few bricks. The house was not finished yet, and now, toward the finish, something could still be done. Satan was absorbed in his thoughts. Then he signaled to one of his demons to approach.

"Azazel," he said, "we must get hold of that soul."

Azazel glanced at the house, frowning. "It will be hard work, my master."

Satan sneered, "Hard, hard. It must be a rare good soul. I shall go down to earth myself and lure it away from God."

"Shall I stand here on guard until you return?"

"Yes, remain here," replied Satan, "be on your guard and follow everything here with attention. When I return you will tell me what you observed. Just watch, I shall descend today and try to get near that person tomorrow, and if the construction of the house stops the day after tomorrow there will be no good deeds down there anymore and no more bricks will move up here. That soul will be ours!"

And with that Satan hurled himself down among the clouds and disappeared into the cold night, like a falling silver star becoming smaller and smaller.

The soul whose good deeds had built the heavenly house was the soul of a poor Jew from Zamosce who owned a grocery on the highway to Lemberg.

Who would have believed that in the whole neighborhood, in the emperor's large Polish province, no Jew was more religious than the little grocer by the highway?

He lived in a tattered old house. There was a store in the front and next to it a shed and pantries. Above the store, a small narrow room, a kind of attic, was built. A miserable looking place, indeed.

His wife and their two children lived in the store, the husband on the upper floor.

When a customer came, the woman served him. Businessmen, wandering peddlers, beggars, and domestic servants—she talked to all of them. She went into the town to shop, kept the store in order, put the flour in sacks, and packed peas and ginger in small, attractive paper cups. Moreover, she reared, nursed, and nurtured the two children.

All that time, the husband sat among his books in the small room on the upper floor studying and praying.

He did not see his wife and children from Sabbath to Sabbath.

He lived in the attic and did not come down, except on Friday evenings. He slept on straw and sat on a hard bench. Each morning his daily provisions were placed in front of the door: bread, vegetables, and water. He lived up there like a prisoner.

The prisoner of God, the Talmud, and the prayerbook.

He was thirty-four. A handsome, blond man. His hair and beard were tangled in curls; on his forehead the furrows, like waves in quicksand, touched one another; and in front of him were the books and the depths of the Talmud. He did not live, he did not breathe for this world. He did not see the glittering spring moon or the autumn frost flowing on the meadow. He studied—studied and prayed. His soul visited the old talmudic academies; it trembled on the benches of Sura and Yamnia; it appeared before the masters in the halls of Nachardea; it listened to Gamaliel and hung with delight on the thundering lips of Akiba; it bowed before the gentle admonition of Joshua ben Chanania and watched with burning eyes the mysterious ways of Simon ben Yochai. He did not see or feel anything that was happening around him; when, after the morning prayer, he buried his head among the pages of the Talmud, his soul fluttered into another millennium. It awakened along the shore of Lake Tiberias, stole into the academy and waited for the *nasi*[13] to start his lecture. He lived in the academy where he debated

the finer points of the Law. He suffered and hid out there
from the Romans. He did not emerge, like a diver, from
the depth of the Talmud to the surface of life until sunset,
when the huge flocks rumbled along the highway and the
bittersweet Polish songs were heard in the evening meadow.

Below the attic, the woman struggled and labored in
the store. She was a true Jewish woman and thus endured
and liked that kind of work. While her husband sat by the
Talmud daydreaming and meditating, or was immersed in
his prayers, the woman waited on customers, counted,
worked, and took care of the two children clutching her
skirt. Only on the sacred day of Sabbath were they all
together, only then did the small door of the attic above the
store open, and only then did he come down, exhausted like
a prisoner from his cell.

But they knew well the reason for that kind of life. It
was the hereafter. The husband knew that while the best
years of his youth were passing, his pious life kept building
a shelter above the clouds, near the Lord. And as the woman
struggled and endured, the ever-present smile on her face
was the sign that she knew it, too.

One day, however, Satan appeared on the highway of
Lemberg, across from the grocery. He stopped, examined
the house and sized up the pious man and his family through
the window.

Satan wore a green traveling suit; he had a sportsman's
hat on his head, a bugle by his side, and a small bag in his
hand. A two-horse carriage stood beside him, slowly following wherever he went.

Satan opened the door of the grocery.

"Good evening, my good woman," he said cheerfully, in
Polish. "I am the emperor's jeweler."

The woman stared at him. What would the emperor's
jeweler want of her?

"I have come," continued Satan, "to buy up all the
precious stones in this area and take them to the emperor.

The emperor's daughter is preparing for her wedding, and we shall make her a wedding dress of diamonds. See how many I have already collected!"

He placed his bag on the old table of the store and opened it. The woman and the two children leaned over it curiously. Suddenly the small store was filled with brightness. The sparkle of opals, rubies, pearls, and diamonds burst forth and lit up the shabby-looking store. The woman drew back and clutched her heart. The wealth of the whole empire glittered in front of her.

Satan smiled. "Don't you have earrings? Don't you have rings, my good woman? Don't you even have a bracelet for sale?"

Pale-faced, the woman shook her head. She had nothing. How beautiful it would have been! She had been yearning for jewelry for so long! How many times her heart had ached for it! She did not have even a pair of earrings.

Her heart and soul were filled with bitterness. When she looked up again Satan was no longer in the store. He had already left.

That night the woman did not sleep. She listened to the endless murmur of prayers coming from above. Her heart was beating fast. Those precious stones, the diamonds of the emperor's jeweler, kept bouncing up and down, glittering in front of her eyes. What wealth, what fabulous treasure! Like a wanderer who had never seen the ocean and stood astonished on the shore of infinity, she stood on the shore of infinity herself, astonished and amazed by the sea of wealth and splendor. Restless and uneasy, she thought of her own sad, oppressed, and poor life. "Is that also possible? Is there another way to live? Is there really anything in the world besides trouble, suffering, and struggle?" she said to herself.

On the following morning, the little boy, who had been playing in front of the store, suddenly ran to his mother. He had found a diamond in the dust of the highway.

No doubt about it. The jeweler must have lost it on the day before when he came to see them. The woman stared at the small glittering stone, turning it over and over in her hands. She felt dizzy looking into its sparkling brilliance. She knew that what she was holding in her hands was worth more than her whole store, the years of struggle, and the house they lived in so miserably poor.

Her small daughter interrupted her thoughts. She had found a sparkling green precious stone while playing on the field next to the store.

The woman put the diamonds down, carefully wrapped them in paper, and ran to the door. She felt great excitement. Her small son and daughter were already searching feverishly in the field, on the highway, and under the trees. It was almost as if the emperor's jeweler had thrown the diamonds away in the neighborhood.

The woman struggled with herself. Should she leave the store alone? She had never done this. It would mean leaving her husband, who was studying and praying, alone. And still—those precious stones—that wealth, those treasures, which were thrown away among the bushes were just waiting to be picked up.

She hesitated for a moment, then left the store. She took a few uncertain steps in the field. The store remained unattended.

As the woman and her two children were searching and picking up diamonds deeper and deeper in the field, Satan appeared at a tree, which had been his hiding place. He looked around and noticed that the husband sat alone in the house. Then he slowly pressed down the doorknob.

It was a strange, interesting moment. Above, was the pious man among his books. Below, in the store, was the devil, smiling.

Satan walked around the racks of shelves. He looked around, searching, and examining. Suddenly he called out in a loud voice, "Hallo there! Is anyone here?"

Above, on the upper floor, the pious man shuddered. Was not his wife in the store? What was that shouting about? But then he went back to his studying.

Satan called out again, "Where is the storekeeper?"

Above, the pious man frowned. What could have happened? Had his wife left the store? He was about to push his book aside. But no, he composed himself and leaned over the book again. Then Satan called out for the third time, "Dammit! I shall carry off this store!"

Above, the pious man frowned again. With sudden decision he stood up, left his books, and walked down the stairs to the store.

In that moment, up in Heaven, the demons who were standing in front of the nearly finished house noticed that the construction came to a halt. It was the moment that the pious man had stood up and left his books. And in that moment, when the pious man interrupted his accustomed way of life, the construction of the miraculous house stopped.

The pious man entered the store. His face was red from fear and anxiety. It must have been an unusual visitor to succeed in disturbing him. And the woman? Where could his wife be?

But she could not be found. Suddenly the pious man and Satan stood face to face. Satan put his hand on the pious man's shoulder. "Is this your store?"

"Yes, master."

"And what were you doing upstairs?"

"I was praying, master. I am a Jew."

"Do you know who I am?"

"No, master, I don't."

The pious man's whole body trembled. He ran his fingers through his blond, disheveled hair. Beads of perspiration appeared on his forehead. He was afraid of the stranger.

Satan jumped on the counter and began to dangle his feet.

"Listen, Jew," he said. "Do you really think that there

is nothing in the world besides books and prayer? Do you believe that you must grow old by the pages of the Talmud, waste your life here, and then be buried in some forgotten village cemetery? Has the world reached its end for you in this miserable store? Is there no highway, and beyond it great, strange lands, splendid gardens, glittering cities? Is there no sea, and are there no ships rocking on it? Are there no palaces, ladies and kings, gold and money, pearls and music— and spring, spring and love?"

The pious man could hardly reply. "I don't know, master."

Satan roared, "You don't know? Well, I do! Why do you go on throwing away your life, your youth? Look at the way you live, Jew! Do you want to waste this one life of yours, which shall never return or be renewed, in this store? And do you want your children to become beggars, like you? Look outside, at the sun, you Jewish storekeeper, and see how the grass grows, how the bushes turn green, how the daisies sprout among the wheat stalks; look at the lizards on the white gravel, see how everything is alive, moving and bursting forth—and you keep sitting in your cubbyhole and studying. For how long? You are thirty years old, you poor Jew, and each day takes you a step closer to your grave. Leave your books, leave the misery, and come with me."

The pious man's answer came in feeble, halting words, "I am God's. I serve only God. You cannot give me anything because God is mine—and that is worth more to me than anything you can offer."

Satan whistled. Outside the wheels of a carriage were heard rolling. Two proud stallions kicked up their hooves in the air in front of the store.

"Do you know who I am?" he sneered at the Jew. "I am the majordomo of the king of France. I have come here by accident. I come from the king of Poland to whom I took a letter from my master. Now, I am on my way home. I just wanted to stop for a while on this highway. But I am on my way. I shall leave you to your fate. I merely wanted to help you—that is to say, not you, because you, poor fellow, it seems, are not quite of sound mind. I would have liked to help your wife and children."

The pious man stared at Satan. "My wife?"

"You could have come with me, in my carriage, you Jewish storekeeper. I could have got goods for your store in my country cheaply, perhaps even for free. My king has a thousand ships sailing the high seas. Each brings figs and dates from the Indies. They all lie in boxes on the shore, unopened and unattended. You could have got many of them for your store. Then you would not have to live in such poverty. But if you don't want to listen to me, it is all right with me."

Having said that, Satan set out toward the carriage, whistling and cracking his whip.

The pious man pressed his hand against his forehead. His heart beat at a feverish pace. The stranger was already at the door. He was about to leap on his carriage. And the goods—and his wife and children—and those fruits from overseas—and the family—the family.

Like a small child picked off the ground, the pious man was lifted into the carriage by Satan. The driver lashed the horses. The next moment, the carriage disappeared at the turn.

The pious man's silk cap lay in the dust of the highway.

The house in which a happy family had once lived stood deserted on the highway. The woman and the children were still searching for the discarded jewels in the fields. And the head of the family, a pious man, was traveling in Satan's arms toward a strange world.

Up there, in the fifth kingdom of Heaven, where pious souls were building their shelters by their good deeds, that nearly-finished house stood quietly in the midst of devils merrily dancing a demonic ring dance.

The zaddik of Kálló broke off his story for a moment.
He looked around. All of them sat around the tavern table
in the dim light of twilight. As they looked at the zaddik,
the faces of the three card players seemed pale. Even his
companions stared at the storyteller. And the zaddik of Kálló
looked out into the Sabbath dawn that began to break above
the steppe. "The story will end soon," he said.

A year had passed since Satan carried away the poor
Jew of Zamosce from his peaceful home. A year later, up
in the fifth kingdom of Heaven, on that wide road where
demons wandered, Azazel and Beliyaal, two young demons,
met.

They wagged their long tails when they noticed each other
and their eyes threw sulphurous flames.

"Have you heard, little brother, what's happened?"
shouted Azazel from afar. "You haven't? Listen well, because
what I am about to tell you is the greatest miracle of
Heaven and earth. Satan has abdicated!"

Beliyaal stood openmouthed. His long, pointed tongue
lolled out in astonishment.

"Satan, our Father and Creator?"

"Yes, the great Satan, our Father and Leader, the great
Ashmodai."

Having said that, they rode on. And more and more
devils learned of the astonishing news. In the great excitement,
their grotesque, black bodies crowded the wide roads of
Heaven where the houses of the happy souls stood and grew
mysteriously. As their dark foreheads shuddered and their
cross eyes became inflamed, the hairy, frightening demons
sweated. Azazel, the youthful demon, ran down the road at
the head of a growing party. Dull and frightening sounds
were heard, as if millstonse had been thrown against one
another, or people were fighting with dull swords, or crudely
filed nails were scratching on velvet. The horrifying noise of

the demons would have been deafening to the ears of mortals and the sounds of their terrible grating would have frightened all grazing animals off the fields.

Suddenly the group of demons stopped in front of a small house. Next to the house, like a scalded, black dog, Ashmodai, the leader of demons, the ancient enemy of everything good, was cringing on the ground. He lay there moaning and occasionally staring painfully with bulging eyes at the house that stood next to him. The house was finished. The house of the Jew from Zamosce.

It was finished, finished completely, ready to be occupied by an earthly soul in any moment. The eternal home was finished in the fifth kingdom of Heaven where the soul was to live in God's splendor and rest to the end of times. The roof was finished and was decorated with silver scales: a scale for each year spent in study and prayer. The gate was laden with emeralds, because he lived on bread and water, pure and unblemished, like a flower in the field. The chamber was made of white marble and there were two silver chairs in it, one for the pious man, the other for his wife. The house was finished down to the last brick; it was a perfect life and a victory for God. A good soul proved that it was worth creating man from the dust of the earth.

And next to it Satan lay moaning and weeping, "I lost the game. I descended upon earth myself in order to entice that soul and thereby prevent the completion of this house. I, myself, yet the house is finished. The angels laughed at me and made fun of me, and the whole Heaven was filled with the ringing of bells. I felt so humiliated that I resigned my office. I have already told the Lord that I would not be Satan any longer. Someone much stronger should become Satan."

He looked over the crowd of demons and pointed to his younger brother.

"Azazel," he said in a feeble voice, "you will be my successor, you will become the new Satan. I am transferring

my office to you. Here are the whistle, the bugle, the fire-
brand, and the lock of Hell."

A red flame started to flash in Azazel's eyes. He leaned
over the fallen Satan, "And how did you make such a mess
of that jump, old man? Perhaps you will tell us so that we
might learn from it."

Ashmodai sighed deeply and pointed to the house in a
fit of rage. "I descended upon earth. I, myself! I tore him
from his wife and children. I made him sit in my carriage and
carried him into the sin of sins, from vice to vice. In the
very moment when he left his books the construction of that
house up here ceased. And I dragged him farther and farther,
and deeper and deeper. We traveled on Sabbaths, on holi-
days. we ate of the forbidden food of peasants, and I began
to think that he had already forgotten everything. He just
sat by me in the carriage, dreaming and meditating. You
could see up here that nothing was added to that house. The
soul had separated from God. I took that Jew to the royal
castle, and he became the supervisor of the king's gardens.
Like a person suffering from sleeping sickness, he was only
half awake as he wandered about in his office issuing orders
and making arrangements. He spoke quietly with the servants
and his trembling hands often touched the pines and the
birches in the well-kept parks. By then he no longer had a
beard. We cut off his blond locks and made him wear a
courtier's uniform. I watched him happily day by day as he
seemed to resign himself to his fate. I did not leave him alone
for a moment and the chief gardener—that was his new
office—the king's chief gardener seemed to have forgotten
his previous life."

Ashmodai paused for a moment but then he went on
disconsolately, "But one day, my sons, he escaped! Through
the wire fence of the palace he noticed a Jew who was on
his way to the synagogue, with his prayer book and sack
under his arms. With his forehead pressed against the fence,
my Jew immediately engaged in a feverish conversation,

questioning the Jew outside. Then he broke through the gate, ran out of the garden and away with the stranger. The remembrance of his past life awakened in him. He recalled his past, his wife and children, his God, his store, and his prayer book. And he escaped. I searched after him in vain for months. Then I returned embittered to the highway of Lemberg. I stopped in front of the house from which I had carried him off. I saw his wife working in the store, and his children playing. He had returned home. He had taken up his studies again. He finished his house up here and saved the heavenly bliss of his soul. And I lost the game forever."

Ashmodai bowed his head. Satan was weeping in his anger.

The demons stood around the fallen leader, stamping in outrage and sympathy for him. Only Azazel, the new chief of the demons, stood insolently and presumptuously in front of Ashmodai.

"Tell me, old man," he said tauntingly. "How old was that Jew of yours?"

"Thirty-two, little brother."

"That was your undoing, old man," sneered Azazel. "Why did you start with such a young one? You can entice one like that to no end; he is still young enough to repent his sins. He can still reform himself and amend his ways. I shall do it differently, you clumsy Ashmodai."

The fallen demon stared at his successor. And Azazel continued, "Differently, that's for sure! I shall start only with old ones, whose hair is already gray and who are past sixty. You can entice them easily, because they have no time to start their lives anew. I shall entice only old people, because they will remain Satan's forever."

Elated by this display of great wisdom, the army of demons burst into happy laughter and proudly danced around the new Satan, Azazel.

And with that, my story is finished.

The zaddik of Kálló rose from the table. It was already

light, perhaps six o'clock in the morning. The sun rose over the Hortobágy[4] in clear brilliance, shedding its golden light on the draw wells.

At first, the whole group sat motionless at the table in astonished silence. Then one of the players, the oldest, staggered to the zaddik and suddenly threw himself to the ground in front of him.

"Rebbe," he exclaimed, "is it still possible? Is it still possible?"

The zaddik of Kálló shrugged his shoulders and looked at the kneeling man. Was it only then that he wanted to repent?

"Is it still possible? Is it always possible," he replied. "We were hurrying to the synagogue. Today is the Sabbath of *Yisro,* and the Ten Commandments will be recited. The Fourth Commandment is about the Sabbath. And before I was about to hear it as it sparkled off the sacred parchment of the Torah, I received a message from the cantor's singing mouth that I should bring you back to the right path, you who broke the Sabbath."

Reb Shayeh Aaron leaped to his feet and continued officiously, "Three messages were sent. The third came as we were sitting at the Sabbath dinner and the zaddik was just explaining the verse 'he who protects the Sabbath from being violated will be greatly rewarded.' Was it not so, Reb Chayyim?"

"It certainly was," nodded Reb Chayyim bravely.

Then it was the second player's turn. His voice was also filled with bitterness. "Rebbe," he sighed, "the three of us are brothers, wine merchants from Tokaj. We used to be pious and God-fearing people, but for the past three months some evil has been harming us. We play cards. We must play cards. We have played throughout the land. We have been winning from each other and from strangers. And we cannot rid ourselves of these demonic cards."

The zaddik looked the two players over, then he turned to the third. "Who was your father?"

"Our father died in Sziget.[15] He had originally come from Zamosce, and our grandfather was a pious and gentle man. Perhaps he was the one of whom the zaddik told his story. And Satan, who could not get the better of our grandfather, has now succeeded in enticing us."

The zaddik touched the heads of the three players. "Come along," he said, "we are going to the synagogue. Let's listen to the Ten Commandments. And you, my brothers, shall be cured."

And with that, all of them walked out of the tavern. The gold and silver coins and the cards remained thrown together on the table. First came the zaddik and, following him, the six Jews—three pious ones and three redeemed sinners.

They reached the turn of the highway. The wire, the Sabbath wire, had been waiting for them patiently. The zaddik touched the wire and said quietly, "Sabbath, Sabbath, I've come because of you and we are returning because of you. Sabbath, Sabbath, the pearl of Israel, God's jewel, watch over us, accompany us, wrap us up in your veil, and love us. Sabbath, Sabbath, peace and rest, take us upon your wings. Amen."

And when he finished saying that, all of them started walking in a miraculous procession on the great highway of Nyiregyháza, toward Kálló.

10

Mayerl

Mayerl Sets Out

"Mayerl, Mayerl, come back in time!"

"I'll be back, mother."

"Mayerl, Mayerl, be careful on the road!"

"I'll be careful, mother."

"Watch out that the horse doesn't kick you, that the komondor doesn't bite you; don't sink into the marsh, don't let the poison ivy make you bleed, Mayerl, Mayerl!"

"I'll walk straight ahead on the highway, mother."

"Avoid the gendarmes, lift your hat to the soldiers, and don't pick a quarrel with the border guards, Mayerl, Mayerl!"

"Don't be afraid for me, mother."

"When will you come back, Mayerl?"

"Before summer, mother."

Then a quiet scream was replaced by sobbing, and a white kerchief fluttered in the window of the small country house. Mayerl stepped out through the gate.

Suddenly a deep, booming voice was heard in the courtyard, "Come here, Mayerl, let me bless you."

Mayerl stopped by the fence. An old, wrinkled hand touched his head. "Remain a Jew, my son. Don't forsake God."

Mayerl wept. He kissed the old hand. His father appeared by the fence. It was the zaddik of Kálló.

156

His beard, which had been white had turned yellow with old age. His face was filled with a thousand wrinkles, deep, sad furrows were on his forehead. The zaddik had grown quite old. "You won't forget me, Mayerl, will you?" he asked.

Mayerl could not even answer; he was ready to break into tears. His father nodded, "It will take you a month to reach Pozsony.[1] By then, it will be cold under the Carpathian Mountains. I am afraid of the cold, my son."

Mayerl was sniveling.

"The winter will carry me away, Mayerl. Perhaps I won't ever see you again on this earth. We shall meet only up there, in front of God's throne. There I shall have to give account of you, too, Mayerl. My soul is pure. I brought you up to serve God. Ever since you could speak, you've been speaking of God. There is nothing in your soul except the joy of God and His light. Whatever I knew of God I poured into you, like an old stream that gives its water to a young springlet. And now I am sending you away because I can teach you no longer. You will go to large cities, large schools, and large synagogues. Don't ever forsake God."

Mayerl's tears were streaming down his cheeks, his shining, small black beard, and his sprouting moustache, down the new black silk kaftan and the small bundle into which some provisions had been packed for the road. He still could not answer.

"And then, little Mayerl, when you have studied a great deal, when you know a great deal, come back here, to Kálló. This is a small village, but it offers happiness, tranquillity, and satisfaction. If you come back young, you'll be my successor. But it might also be that you'll come back an old, graying man. Then go to the cemetery, to my grave and your mother's grave. Pray there for yourself and for the happiness of your soul. And remember, nowhere will your tired body be soothed by such tranquillity as in the old cemetery of Kálló."

Words finally came to Mayerl. "Rebbe," he said haltingly,

"my dear father, I would like to come home to Kálló by next summer."

The zaddik just kept looking at his only son. "Mayerl," he said, "take this *kamea* with you."

It was an amulet wrapped in red silk, a wonder-working thing. The zaddik often gave such magic talismans to those who had made a pilgrimage to see him. He gave small gold coins to some, silver medallions to others, or small boxes covered with precious stones, and pieces of parchment hanging on green ribbons on which kabbalistic sayings and letters shaped in the form of a lion's head could be seen. But that *kamea* must have been an unusual thing. The zaddik gave that to his own son.

Mayerl's hands trembled as he unwrapped the silk cover. Suddenly, he looked startled. The amulet was no more than a small rectangular mirror. There was no ornament, no embellishment on it. Slurred red paint on its back; on its face, nothing.

Only a mirror.

Mayerl looked up, but the rebbe had already disappeared into the house. He shook himself; he was ready for the journey. He placed the amulet in its silk cover and put it in his pocket. Then he set out toward the street. Forward, into the world!

It was drizzling with the September rain. The dust settled on the streets of Kálló. The sagging locust trees that stood on both sides of the street were already turning yellow. Here and there faces appeared in the windows greeting the young wanderer. The bashful eyes of young Jewish girls glittered through the white curtains; and old Jews waved to him with big clumsy gestures. Mayerl walked slowly, then turned at the corner. He stood by the *cheder*. Loud humming, like the monotonous song of little bees, could be heard outside. Mayerl looked in through the window. The small Jewish boys of Kálló were studying. The song of the choir was ascending and little heads with earlocks were bouncing from side to side. They were singing the sacred text of Moses, occasionally interrupted by Rashi,[2] for without those commentaries there could be no study. *"Fregt Rashe,"*[3] the teacher's voice was heard. He slammed his reed stick on the table and, like a wave let loose, fifty voices echoed Rashi's question and answer. It was like the waters of the sea slamming against rocks. Suddenly the humming stopped. Like the waters of the sea broken up by a defiant rock, chaotic sounds were heard. An obstacle had come up unexpectedly. A rock on the straight path. A reef in the open sea. But a *weizerl* emerged from Rashi's text; a guide. It was a difficult sentence, a few incomprehensible words that interrupted the smoothly-flowing text, words by which the master had wanted to explain a great deal, but they were so difficult to comprehend that even those whose excellence in talmudic study was well known pointed at them as if they were rare finds. The children came to a standstill, like hikers attempting to climb a peak, then slowly and carefully approached the weighty words of the *weizerl.*

The son of the zaddik of Kálló sighed and walked on. That *cheder* had been his childhood. Other boys would bid farewell to the forest, the park, the reed sticks, the wooden loop. For him the *cheder* meant all that. Four dingy walls, a tired old teacher, and Moses and Rashi. Farewell, poor, sad, little school; greetings, real life, wisdom—true wisdom.

He first walked on the highway, then among fields and meadows, sinking knee-deep in the grass or among the crops. The light wind of the steppe caressed his fourteen-year-old head. Mayerl looked at the flowers, and started daydreaming. He recalled one of his father's tales that he had heard from him as a child. The flowers, so said the zaddik, were also God's servants. Among them, too, there were faithful, pious, zealous, and God-fearing ones. Flowers, so taught the zaddik, were better than people. Flowers prayed better and more beautifully than people. God loved flowers more than people, and it was for that reason that He sent their rain on time—

the gentle dew. The prayers of people were rarely answered. They had to wait for rain for weeks and often in vain. Flowers, however, received their rain in the morning and in the evening, and when they lowered their bells in order to accept it, they sighed a prayer of gratitude.

Mayerl kept looking at the flowers. The quiet little violet was a hasid, his father once told him, a pious, religious soul. It folded inward by drawing its petals together when it was praying. Swinging recklessly and angrily in the air, the poppy was an *apikores*, an unbelieving and ungodly flower, afraid of nothing. But how long was its life? The wind came and tore off its petals in a moment. The sunflower was a *purets*, a great noble. It looked at the sky arrogantly as if it said, "I, only I, ask for nothing!" Standing next to it, as if begging for *tzedokoh*, for alms, were the two beggars—the battered boxtree and the sad widow, the poor cornflower. The *purets* did not even look at them. The mignonette was the scholar of the flowers, the *talmid chochom*. How it swung left and right, watching over its neighbors!

The flowers made Mayerl think of his life. Should he look at the flowers the same way he used to watch people in the synagogue of Kálló? Was he going to remain a Talmudist for the rest of his life and nothing else? Was there nothing in the world but prayer, study, the Sabbath, and ancient sacred books? Were there no great cities with glittering palaces, carriages, kings, and princes? Were there no young ladies, girls, and women like the ones he had seen driving through one of the streets of Kálló when the provincial assembly was in session? Was not his life going to be different from what it had been so far? Where did that road lead, anyway? From Kálló to Pozsony; from one school to another. No sooner had he closed one book than he had to open another. In Kálló, only his father watched over him; in Pozsony, the whole Jewish quarter would guard his steps.

Mayerl's expression turned serious. He sighed deeply; he was alone on the road. He was free. There he could think. He lay down in the grass.

"What is going to become of you, Mayerl?" he mused. "Your father brought you up to be a rabbi. Did you observe the life he lived?"

A life full of wonder, full of misery. Half of the country came to him for counsel, half of the country asked him for medicine, cure, and escape in times of difficulty. Look at your father, Mayerl! How ill, old, and poor he is! Whatever he had in his soul, he gave to the despondent. Whatever he had in silver, he distributed among the poor. What did he have left? An old wooden bed and a bookcase. Now he lives there, suffering in his old age. Was it worth it? And your mother, Zese, the *rebbetsen,* doesn't even have a decent silk scarf. Is that the life you want to live, Mayerl?

Horrified, Mayerl jumped to his feet. It was as if Satan had tempted him. The land around him was silent; there was no one around him. He lay alone in the field. He almost ran as he got up. He wanted to run from his thoughts; sweat poured down his forehead, although the sun was already setting. He ran toward the Tisza.

The wheels of a carriage clattered behind him in the late afternoon. A carriage, not a peasant's wagon. A kind of coach. The black coach was swaying gently on the high spokes as the coachman guided a large stallion. Mayerl stopped, allowing it to catch up with him. As the coach passed by him, a girl leaned out smiling. Mayerl turned pale. He had never seen anything so beautiful: golden hair, eyes blue like a forget-me-not, a pink ribbon across the white forehead. As if he had looked into the sun, Mayerl lowered his eyes. There was so much pain and despair written on his face that the blond girl leaned out even more and then a clear voice rang out, "Mother! Mother! Some poor, wandering Jew-boy is standing on the road. Couldn't we pick him up?"

The coach stopped with a sudden jolt. Joyous laughter was heard outside. An elderly lady leaned out. "Where are you going, young man?" she asked Mayerl.

"To Pozsony, milady," stammered Mayerl.

"We could take you part of the way if you won't take offense at it," said a man's voice mixed with laughter.

"Sit by the coachman, I can see you are exhausted," said the girl with the golden hair.

Mayerl felt dizzy. He bowed toward the coach and dropped his bundle. And then—even he did not know how—he climbed up and sat by the coachman. The coach started moving again.

Inside, the laughter did not stop. And then, in order that those in the driver's seat might not hear it, the voices started whispering.

"What's the idea with the Jew, Clarissa?"

"I am taking him to the bishop. The Bishop of Várad[4] is dining with us tonight. He loves such presents."

Again laughter. Then the hushed conversation continued.

"And how are you going to take him to the castle?"

"We'll tell him to sleep there tonight."

"He is very dirty, poor—"

"The Bishop of Várad will bathe him."

Mayerl just sat, dazed and exhausted. The long day's wandering, walking, and meditating had made him weary. He leaned against the driver, who smiled but said nothing. They rode at full speed on the great steppe of Szabolcs. But where, who knew? Mayerl fell asleep in the driver's seat.

In his deam, his small child's soul flew to his father. He sat in front of the old zaddik studying a large book of the Talmud. He saw his mother as she leaned over him, and half asleep he felt faintly that they were driving through a big gate and that he was carefully taken off the driver's seat and carried off somewhere.

When he opened his eyes, he saw two men standing at his bed in a large, elaborately furnished room. Both wore long priestly robes. One had a wrinkled, old face and wore a purple belt around his waist. The younger, tall and thin, stood behind him. Mayerl just stared at them; he felt that he was still dreaming.

"What is your name, my son?" asked the one with the purple belt.

"Mayerl," the boy whispered.

Then he closed his eyes and fell into a deep, deep sleep.

Mayerl Awakens

It was getting dark in the great marshes of the Tisza. The air was filled by an unusual chaos of voices. The long, sad cry of spoonbills, the screaming of peewits, and the concert of frogs and grasshoppers blended in a sad wave of sounds. It stopped for a moment when the evening express train from Nyiregyháza appeared at the turn in the direction of the village of Tiszadada[5] and ran along the embankment whistling hoarsely. It was only then that every kind of animal inhabiting the marshes stuck out is head. The frogs blinked at the monster with the fiery eyes and the wild geese flew up, angrily flapping their wings. Then the steaming train disappeared and the concert of the marshes began anew filling the peaceful night above the steppe of Szabolcs.

The sound of angry shouting was heard on the highway when the red eyes of the train disappeared among the poplars "Dammit! We missed the train! What's going to happen to you now, you shabby Jews?"

The shouting came from a huge figure, the gendarme, and one of the best. An officer, judging by his rank. He walked on the highway at the head of an unusual group. Old, shrunken, ragged figures marched in line behind him, men and women, carrying bundles and packs and leaning on big staffs. Here and there one of them fell out of line, but six gendarmes were there with their guns and kept order in the strange troop. They were beared, old Jewish men and tattered, ragged, Jewish women. They were beggars.

When the officer pointed to the departing train, there was commotion among the beggars, "We aren't going any farther!

Take us back to Tiszalök![6] We're tired!"

They were all shouting and demanding, but the gendarmes started working them over with the butts of their guns. The officer yelled, "Silence, Jews, I tell you! I wanted to get on the train at Királytelek[7] to get to the county hall, but we missed the train on account of your weak legs, and now we'll have to walk to Nyiregyháza. If I can take it, so can you. I want to hand you over to Judge Bary by morning."

"But what did we do to break the law?" shouted a stoop-shouldered figure.

The officer twirled his moustache and said, "I won't tell you that, you'll hear it from the judge. His Excellency will find among you the one who helped in the killing of Eszter Solymosi in Eszlár."[8]

Like a lake stirred by the waves of a pebble thrown into it, the words aroused great excitement in the group. Fists rose and curses flew in the air. They wanted to crowd in front of the officer to swear their innocence, but the gendarmes held them back. Then they started marching. The officer marched with a soldierly posture. Behind him in the dust of the road, under the dark sky, went the twenty-six beggars and the six gendarmes. Some of the older beggars were praying the evening prayer amid tears, and burst into more tears at the verse *hayshieni Elayhe yisheyni* (Help us, God of our saving). There was also some among them who, nearly collapsing from pain, started reciting the lamenting song of *Tisho Beov*,[9] *Zehayr me hoyo lonu habito uree es cherposeyni* (Look down upon us God and see what has happened to us and look upon our terrible shame). One of the gendarmes kept whistling a Hungarian tune. Whenever they caught sight of an approaching cow carrying water buckets, the women pressed their way to the front gasping, and begged the gendarme for some water.

They had been walking through the marshland in that manner for half an hour. Suddenly one of the gendarmes ran to the head of the column and asked permission to speak with the officer. "I am reporting, sir, that a very old Jew has just collapsed and is lying on the road unconscious."

The officer ran back. So it was. An old man lay in the dust, stretched out like a corpse. He had been caught that morning on the highway between Eszlár and Nagyfalu.[10] He carried no money or documents identifying him. A beggar, of course! The lining of his kaftan was torn open, his beard was disheveled, and one of his hands was bleeding from the gentle touch of a gun's butt. He was unconscious. Did he faint from the heat of the sun, hunger, or exhaustion? Who knew? He had not been given anything to eat or drink since his capture. They searched his pockets for perhaps a piece of bread or a spirit flask. They found nothing in them except a battered old prayer book. That was his sole possession.

An old, unconscious Jew lying on the highway. What could be done for him?

The others could barely drag themselves. They were completely exhausted by the cruel pace of the march. Some already sat dazed by the road. These men had to be housed somewhere for the night, otherwise they would surely perish. And the officer's order did not call for dead Jews to be carried to the judge; he had to deliver live Jews.

The officer looked around. They were on the open road between the farmlands of Hajnalos and the town of Görögszállás. There was a small, marshy, drying lake ahead of them. On the shore of the lake was the Castle of Hajnalos. There were lights, it seemed, in its windows.

Few people knew much about the Castle of Hajnalos. They knew that it belonged to the Kállays. Its owner was one of the farm-bailiffs of the Kállay family, a relative of one of the collateral branches. He was also a Kállay, a retiring, severe old man. For decades, the people recalled, he had not been to a county assembly, a hunt with greyhounds, or to the fall fox hunt. He was absent from the winter balls of the Majláths and the summer picnics of the

Kornisses.[11] He lived withdrawn in his castle with his sick, old wife and only son. The son was blind.

The officer straightened his uniform. He would try the Castle of Hajnalos. He would ask the owner's permission to place that whole fine group in the cellar for the night. After all, he was an aristocrat, a Hungarian nobleman, and a Kállay at that. It would not be difficult to make him understand that, according to the law, those beggar Jews had to be taken to Nyiregyháza in good condition.

The gendarmes roused the beggars, "On your feet, Jews! We are going to look for a place to sleep."

The beggars lifted the unconscious old man and carried him. The group waded through a few puddles and circled the marshy lake before reaching the castle.

The entrance, like the gate of a fortress, was dark. Behind the bars stood a densely planted row of poplars, concealing freely roaming dogs ready to charge at the smell of a stranger. The officer looked into the darkness and noticed the glow of a pipe in front of the gate. He walked there hurriedly.

The man smoking was the owner of the castle.

As could be distinguished by the flashing sparks, he was a huge old man. His beard was white and thick. He wore a hat and a leather coat. He was taking big puffs of his pipe. The officer stood before him and introduced himself. "András Recsky, district officer, at your service."

The old man nodded. "Kállay," he replied coldly.

The officer continued undisturbed, "I was ordered to pick up Jewish beggars in my district, Your Excellency. I must take them to the county jail. We missed the evening train, and a few collapsed from fatigue. If it is not offensive to Your Excellency, let us rest here in the Castle of Hajnalos tonight. I would put the beggars in the cellar. As for myself, I'll even sleep on a bench here in the garden."

The pipe flared up a few times. Heavy rings of smoke went up. The answer came in a deep, heavy voice, "I don't mind. Take them down to the cellar. I'll have some water brought to them. And officer, you'll be my guest for dinner."

The key of the Castle of Hajnalos turned the old lock of the cellar. The wide iron door opened. It bore the coat of arms of the Kállay family. The beggars dragged down the wide staircase and threw themselves on the cold stones. Water was brought to them in large buckets from the kitchen. The beggars fell on them and in their great thirst drank the water to the last drop. The unconscious old Jew was laid out in a separate recess of the cellar. A gendarme remained with him and asked for plum brandy as he attempted to revive him.

Above, on the terrace of the castle, among the trees, on the second floor, supper was prepared for two. There they sat, the master of the castle and across from him the tulip-red-cheeked, fearsome officer with his pointed moustache. Neither the wife nor son of the host was present. Both had been ill for years.

The two sat at the lonely table. The wine bottle clanked, and the good *homoki*[12] yellow wine was poured into tall glasses. Large buzzing mosquitoes kept bumping into the glass of the garden lamp and an occasional foolish dragonfly flew through a narrow opening into the flames and burned to ashes amid loud crackling. The night wind blew gently, and Officer András Recsky lit a cigar.

"You know, Your Excellency," he started explaining to the owner of the castle, "the fact of the matter is, that besides the Jews of the village, a wandering Jewish beggar was also present at the murder of Eszlár. It was he who led Eszter by the hand into the synagogue and held the girl while they took her blood."

A huge cloud of smoke went up from the pipe. "Could that foolish story be true?" said the host.

András Recsky was astonished. He had never heard a comment like that coming from a Hungarian nobleman. He twirled his moustache, "Well, begging your pardon, Your Excellency, the whole of Hungary is on fire and the whole world knows that the Jews murdered Eszter Solymosi. Don't you read the papers, Your Excellency? How can you live here in your castle so quietly when for more than half a year people in your district have been speaking of nothing but that Jewish disgrace?"

The host pushed up his hat. A high, noble forehead framed by gray hair became visible. He passed his hand across his forehead as if to make a pressing thought disappear, then lifted his pipe again. "Officer," he said, "I haven't read a paper in ten years. I nurse my sick wife and son and manage the affairs of my estate. You are the first stranger who has visited me in a long time. All I know about the case of Eszlár is what I occasionally hear my farm workers and servants tell one another during work. But that's like folktale. I have never believed it. Who would believe that there was a mysterious, wandering, Jewish stranger or that in broad daylight a peasant girl was dragged into the synagogue to be cut to pieces? I believe that Eszter Solymosi drowned herself in the Tisza because her mother had beaten her. She'll be fished out before the river freezes over."

András Recsky was so astonished that he dropped his cigar. He had never heard anything like that. Not even the paid Christian defenders of the Jews wrote such things in the Jewish newspapers. How could a Hungarian nobleman have an opinion like that!

The master of the castle bent over and picked up the officer's cigar. "And what do these beggars have to do with that affair?" he asked firmly.

Officer András Recsky looked defiantly into his host's eyes. He took a swig of his drink and slammed down the glass.

"I picked up the beggars during the last three days in the vicinity of Eszlár and Nagyfalu, Your Excellency. We must find that wandering Jewish beggar who took part in the killing of Eszter Solymosi. A beggar like that does not wander far off. He usually nestles in an area for as long as a year without leaving his hiding place. I had all of those ragged Jewish beggars in that area picked up. I shall take them to Judge Bary. He will pick out the guilty one. And even if the killer isn't among them, one of them should be able to give us information about him. The truth will be out in the jail in Nyiregyháza, which neither the Jews' money nor the Rothschilds' gold can reach. It is regrettable that instead of helping to rid this blessed land of the Jews, such a level-headed Hungarian gentleman like you, Your Excellency, takes their side without knowing how guilty they all are. I know, Your Excellency. If it were up to me, I wouldn't leave one here, even as a specimen. Let them clear out of here to Palestine, that hellish breed. You've got to deal with them as I used to and I have done now when I cleaned those ragamuffins out of of their holes. I dragged them away as they were eating lunch and supper, pulled them out of the synagogues, and caught them on the highway. The reason that I let them rest is that they may regain their strength by the time they get to Judge Bary. He wants those Jews fresh, not unconscious!"

The clouds of smoke coming from the pipe became larger and thicker. They completely covered the host's face. Suddenly, quiet and careful steps were heard shuffling on the terrace. The stooping figure of the castle's chief steward appeared at the table. "Your Excellency," he said slowly, "there is a very old man down there among the prisoners. He was unconscious when he was brought here. And now, it seems, he's nearing his end. I've tried to revive him, but it's no use. He cannot be brought back to life. While gasping for breath, he kept repeating that he had something to tell you, Your Excellency."

András Recsky filled up his glass. "I'll go down at once and silence that old fool," he said heatedly.

The host rose from his seat. He put down his pipe. He motioned the officer to stay and put another bottle in front of him. Then he turned to the chief steward, "I'll see what that beggar wants. Let's go, old man."

There was a dilapidated small partition in the Castle of Hajnalos. It was filled with cracked barrels, crumbling staves, and rusty clamps. The old man was laid out on the top of a pile of shavings. A nightlight flickered above his head and next to him a yawning gendarme stood. Beyond the thin wall the beggars whom András Recsky's gendarmes had rounded up slept on canvases laid out on the cold floor.

The owner of the castle had to bend down in order to step into the small partition. When he felt the visitor standing by him, the beggar opened his eyes. They were large, dark, suffering eyes. He stretched out his hands and placed it on the owner's gray head. Then he muttered quietly and incomprehensibly, "The mirror . . . where is the mirror?"

The owner of the castle glanced toward the chief steward. "The dying man is asking for some mirror. Bring down a mirror from the castle."

The chief steward left, and the two men remained alone.

The old beggar pushed himself up by one hand and leaned closer to the master of the castle. "I am asking about *that* mirror, that certain mirror. You probably don't even recall it, but I knew that mirror very well and also the man who gave it to you."

The beggar fell back. There was heavy silence in the dark cellar. Behind the wall the sleeping beggars were moaning in their horrifying dreams. The master of the Castle of Hajnalos stood motionless by the dying old man, listening to his words. The old man spoke with his eyes closed. "They are persecuting and harming us again, and they are rounding us up like hungry dogs; they are after us and we are hungry and thirsty—*shaas nisoyon:* the hour of tribulation is upon us again. The land is on fire, they are preparing against us and they want to destroy us. The fire is burning under our feet and the sky has become heavy like lead. Oh! What's to become of us? Charges and curses are in abundance and there is no one to refute them; the stain of shame and disgrace is upon all of us. Is there no truth? Will the truth never come? Is your soul untroubled, you great lord beside me? Are you not shaking also, like the flower on the bottom of the sea when the storm rages above? Tell me, tell me, doesn't hatred hurt you? Don't you feel anything, master of Hajnalos?"

The owner of the Hajnalos castle did not move. Beads of perspiration appeared on his forehead. His voice was hoarse. "Who are you and what do you want from me?"

The beggar continued without opening his eyes, "And now the fire has reached your house, too. They brought Jews here. Their tormentor wants to torture them here tonight. In *your* house, Your Excellency. Is your soul still healthy? Can you still remember? Or will you permit it? Will you permit in your house the sound of Jews, of innocent, poor people crying? Listen to me, Your Excellency. I know you and I knew your father. I am an old wanderer on this earth. If I die today this way, I shall return to you in a new form tomorrow. Those who know me and my name know that I have been watching over Israel for thousands of years; I appear wherever they are persecuted and die wherever they perish. I am that old Jewish beggar whom everybody persecutes and who lives forever. I suffer with them in this struggle, too. I sat in the jail of Nyiregyháza and stayed up with those unfortunate ones in the night of suffering. I stood on the road to Eszlár and comforted those who had been unjustly harmed. I was your father's friend, I helped him throughout his life, and I appeared on the steppe of Szabolcs when he needed me. I've been a friend of your kind for a long, long time. Believe me, Your Excellency!"

The beggar straightened up. He was shaking with fever. He embraced and pulled the master of the Hajnalos castle closer toward him. "Do you remember? Is your soul awakening? Or are you still asleep? You slept sixty years ago, too. They had taken you to a strange castle. They laid you down.

When you awakened they put new clothes on you. They took away everything you had with slow, evil work. They took away your religion. They made you forget your past. They gave you a new religion, a new name. You were still a child. You forgot everything. Like a person who is asleep. And they gave you land, a castle, a woman, a beautiful blond woman, and you remembered nothing. Do you believe me? Is the sun rising in your soul? I am telling you, everything until now has been a dream. You have slept for sixty years, and now I have come to awaken you in a time of danger. Wake up, wake up, Mayerl."

The master of the Hajnalos castle was shaking. He stuttered as he repeated, "Mayerl? Mayerl?"

The beggar smiled happily, "Yes, that's right. That's your real name—Mayerl. Do you remember now? The Bishop of Várad baptized you and took you to live with him for many, many years, and you forgot your name and religion in strange schools. Mayerl! That's your name. I knew you when you were a child; I saw you studying; I saw you when you wavered; and I saw you leaving. I was a good friend of your father. Do you remember your father? The old zaddik of Kálló? The small house you left forever? Your mother, who cried much for you, until she died? Mayerl, Mayerl, you did not take good care of yourself. You got lost. The priest, the new religion, and the new woman enticed you. But now you can put everything right. I shall go to see your father today, where he is shining brightly among the zaddikim and tell him that I awakened you. Mayerl, wake up! Come back, awaken from the deep sleep. Don't permit your kind to be harmed in your house. Save these unfortunate ones from their tormentors tonight. Mayerl, throw away your lordly robe, throw away your new name, and take your place among the beggars. Amend your ways, as long as you have time left, before it's too late. And now I am going to your father in Heaven and tell him about you."

The beggar fell back, his voice choked, and his words

were almost inaudible, "And the mirror. Find the mirror, Mayerl!"

Heavy steps rumbled down the staircase. The chief steward came. In his hand was a toilette mirror in the French style. Behind him was a gendarme, and someone else who smelled of wine. He stopped in front of the dying beggar and kicked the wall with his boot. "A short night of interrogation won't hurt them, Your Excellency. Come on Jews! Wake up! Let's talk about what happened in Eszlár."

It was András Recsky, the officer. His eyes flashed with a wild light but he gave the master of the Hajnalos castle an affable look.

The master of the Hajnalos castle had just straightened up from the beggar's body. There were tears glittering in his eyes. He frowned and raised his clenched fists. Like a sleepwalker, he took a few uncertain, staggering steps toward the officer and his voice burst out hoarsely from his throat, "András Recsky! Officer of rascals! Tormentor of Jews! Get out! Get out of my house!"

Mayerl Returns Home

What will remain of the summer and the hot days? What will become of the rose after its petals have turned yellow? Where will the splendor of gardens disappear? What will remain of life when our hands begin to shake and our hearts begin to beat more slowly? And of love, when the soul becomes weary?

Is it possible to start life afresh?

Can you say that it was only a dream? Is it possible to grab a new cane, to return to the road, and continue walking on? Sixty years flew by, sixty years, and you say it was only a dream? They stole your faith but now you are going to find it. They stole your name but now you are going after it. You are setting out. You will throw your whole life away and start it afresh. You have a wife; you will forget her. Your son, you will not bother with him any longer. Your castle and estate, you will not mind them. Your name is Mayerl. You will have to continue where you left off when you were fourteen. Your father gave you his blessing and your mother cried for you. Can you betray them? You left for great schools and wise masters. Now you will have to continue on that path. But is it possible, is it possible? Is your heart the same as the heart that was beating then, Mayerl? Is that hand, your lordly hand, the same as the hand that held the walking cane. Are you still alive? Can you go on?

Is it possible to start life afresh?

Who is going to believe you, Mayerl? You are an old Hungarian nobleman who knows nothing about being a Jew, not even a single letter of the Hebrew alphabet. Can you become a pupil in school? What are you going to do?

You chased the officer out of your castle. His men are gone. You gave the Jewish beggars their freedom back. You listened to that mysterious old man who shattered your life in the middle of the night in your cellar and told you who you really were. Did he lie? Even the dying may lie. Look, the other beggars say he was God's man. No one knew him or his name; he appeared among them suddenly, as they say the prophet Elijah does. And when you returned to the cellar looking for him, wanting to close the lifeless eyes, he could not be found anywhere. There are some who say he dragged himself away in the night. Others say he disappeared like *Elye nove*. He comes and goes on earth like a silvery cloud of stars.

Was it true what he said? Did a mysterious distant memory open in your soul like the water lily at midnight below the surface of the Tisza? Do you remember what happened to you as you stood by the dying man? Why did your brain become feverish? Why did your hands tremble?

What kind of forgotten scene brightened up deep in your eyes? Something they made you give up. Something you forgot. At Nyiregyháza they are interrogating Móric, the son of the kosher butcher of Eszlár. In two months, they made him forget his parents. You weren't even as old as Móric when you fell into the hands of the Bishop of Várad. And for sixty years, no one spoke with you about your forgotten past. They placed the large, heavy building of sixty years on your childhood. But you already remember, don't you? You can see your father's eyes as you run out into the night bareheaded, into the dark, into the strange world.

Where, Mayerl, where?

There are no stars in the sky. Do you want to be a beggar, too? You want to wander, you want to bury those sixty years. You are searching for your father; will you find him? You reach his grave on a sad autumn day. You rush feverishly into the vault where his beloved remains lie. You look at his tombstone. You look at it but you cannot read it. You cannot read the Hebrew letters. You throw yourself upon it, asking, crying, and imploring; but the grave does not answer. Your father's grave! The grave does not recognize you. There are some pious men praying at the grave and you ask them. They answer you, but you cannot understand their speech. They are speaking in Yiddish. And as you drag yourself up the stairs, shattered and sobbing, a beam falls out of the wall and crushes one of your legs. On your father's grave! As if your father's fist smashed you in the face. And you continue walking toward the streets of Kálló, bleeding and limping.

Where, Mayerl, where?

You are searching for the house in a Kálló street, but you don't remember. You are searching and asking, but everyone laughs at you. Mayerl? Yes, the zaddik of Kálló had a small son at one time. But he died in a faraway land a long time ago. Who is going to believe you, who do not

know even a line from the Sayings of the Fathers? Could
you be the zaddik's son? They will think you are mad.

And then you wander alone, limping and half-mad, in
strange cities. You hang on the words spoken in the depths
of synagogues, but you don't comprehend them. You listen
to scholars and rabbis but you cannot understand them.
You catch an occasional thought from their discussion, you
learn an occasional melody, and you hope it is still possible.
But you also feel your heart growing weaker and your eyes
hazier. Then you think of home, the deserted castle, the
sick wife, and the blind child—and again your father, your
mother, and the past, and you go on. You suffer and struggle
in the depths of small Hungarian ghettos; you sleep on the
benches of parks at night. You walk the streets in the mornings and observe every face, catch every audible word, like
a young student who wants to learn at any cost. Mayerl,
how much longer?

Is it possible to start life afresh?

Is it possible to say nothing happened, my name is a
small boyish, childish name, Mayerl? I want to study. I want
to pray. I want to amend my ways. Is it possible to make
springtime out of broken branches? It is autumn, it is
autumn, Mayerl. And you keep on wandering. From Huszt[13]
to Sziget, from Sziget to Ujhely. And then to Debrecen.
You keep walking, staring, and hoping. You are tired and
can barely drag yourself.

Like Koheleth, once king of Israel, whom nobody knew
or would believe and who walked alone in a strange world.

In Debrecen, Jews were gathering around the small
synagogue of the hasidim on Csók Street. One after the
other, they appeared through the dark fog in their flowing
kaftans. They talked in the courtyard for a minute, then,
one after the other, they entered bent over—the wooden
door was cut low—into a tent. There were yellow leaves on
the roof, torn chains made of colored paper hanging on its
walls, and many *lulovs*,[14] turned brown and thrown over the

crossbeam, were tossing about. There was rustling; old, sad myrtles were breathing forth fragrance and on the foliage, through the cracks of the *sukkoh*,[15] the cool evening breeze was blowing. On the table was a large candelabrum—it must have been brought there from some Polish city—with flickering lights in its arms. Around the table, Jews were sitting in silence. It was the night of *Hoshano Rabbo*.[16]

The pious were keeping vigil down here and the angels were doing the same up there. And those big heavenly books, whose pages are of red fire, their letters of black fire, their binding of flames and smoke, emerge from Heaven. Those big books that contain the name of every mortal are closed for a whole year on that night. The huge gates, through which the prayers of repenting souls swarm before the Lord, turn in their corners with a loud, heavy grinding, and close. On that night, on that mysterious night, the fate of the world is settled. The Jews sat in the tent keeping vigil with trembling soul.

The flame crackled, and the prayer rose quietly and mysteriously, *"Lochen boni, kaaniyyim al ha-pesach doyfkim* —Our God, like the poor in front of the door, we are standing, knocking, beseeching and reading Your sacred Torah. Have mercy upon us for the sake of the Torah, for the sake of Your sacred book, for the sake of its letters, for the sake of its chapters, and for the sake of the secret that is hidden in its sentences."

The reading of the Torah began—the fifth and most sacred book of Moses. The summary of all events. The splendid garden of all laws. The opal-filled diadem of all commandments.

The leaves crackled from time to time, the candle was burning low, and the heads of those who were keeping vigil were bent down. Then it seemed as if a cool shadow moved across the tent. Someone was walking nearby. Who would tempt the servants of the Lord in that sad, autumn night? Perhaps the spirits, the secret guests of Jewish tents, walked on the yellow leaves, sighing. Perhaps Satan's steps were heard as he was sneaking around the pious hoping to entice them.

There were fifteen hasidic Jews keeping vigil in the tent. The oldest among them was Reb Chayyim Szüszmann, the scholarly rabbi, who had come to Debrecen from Kaba.[17] He was a wise, learned man, God's servant. He knew the secrets but was also well informed on worldly matters. He was restless and worried that night. He kept looking up excitedly from the old *chummash*.[18] He kept pulling on his beard and had just put down his glasses when suddenly he heard the sound of heavy steps in the deserted courtyard.

They were tired, limping steps.

The door opened. The planks cracked and the candles almost blew out in the rush of air. A stranger entered the tent.

For a moment he was barely visible. Only later could his features be made out: a sickly, gray head and a bushy beard. The stranger took a few limping steps and greeted the Jews. Reb Chayyim Levi Szüszmann looked at him, *"Wer zind ir, yid?"*[19]

Another Jew took a step toward him. He spoke to him in Hungarian. The stranger gave him an imploring look and said, "Let me sit down, my brothers. I'd like to rest awhile. I am tired. I have nowhere to go tonight."

Reb Chayyim Szüszmann nodded. The stranger sat down and looked dreamily into the lights of the seven-armed candelabrum. Then the humming sound of praying started again and trembling heads bent over the sacred books. The rabbi looked at the stranger, *"Kennt ihr ka ivre?"*[20]

The stranger sighed, "I understand your language, at times, but I know only Hungarian. I can follow your prayers, but I cannot pray. I've forgotten everything—a great deal."

Reb Chayyim Szüszmann looked at the tired and mournful face and nodded again. He had known cases like that. He must be a repenting Jew who had sinned a great deal.

Let him sit in the tent. Let his soul be refreshed. And they went on praying.

When the last star of the Big Dipper passed its midnight course, the rabbi rose in the dimly lit tent. He stood by the candelabrum; the flickering light covered his fine, black beard and serious face. He raised his hands in the direction of the others and began to speak, "Rebboysem, my dear brothers, do you know what night is tonight? It is the night of death. Up there our fate is decided upon and we are sitting here in this small tent like those condemned to death in their cells. Let us act like those who must die tomorrow and bow ourselves before God's eternal will. My brothers, it has been handed down to us by our great rabbis that on this night, after midnight, those keeping vigil in tents should make a confession aloud and everybody should tell in front of all the others about his gravest sin. Look into your soul and search and let every one of us reveal his gravest sin. As it is written: *Es chatoay ani mazkir*."[21]

An old man who had been standing in the right corner, his body shaking and swaying as during prayer, then began his confession, in a weeping voice, bowing and pounding his chest. "Last year, at my daughter's wedding, a beggar appeared. But I accosted him and chased him away. I didn't know who he was. Oh! If I had only known! My son-in-law died on the wedding night and we buried him two days later. God had sent that beggar in order to test us in the hour of happiness and we could not stand the test."

Another sad voice continued on the other side, "Oh! May God strike me down for the multitude of my sins and vices! I had been rich but became poor. I didn't listen to the teachings of Moses and I accepted a poor widow's last dress as security. On the next day, when I was told that she had gone into hiding in her shame, punishment had already overtaken me. My son, my only son, drowned in the Tisza. Only his suit, his beautiful, clean suit, was brought back by fishermen—as if the Lord had sent a message. He sent me a suit in return for its kind."

Sobbing, crying, wailing, and moaning filled the dark tent. Everybody was preparing for the declaration of sins. Faces, watered with tears, were pressed together. The night was filled with noise and clamor. Suddenly the lame stranger stood up and shouted in a quivering voice, "It is my turn! It is my turn!"

Everybody rushed to his side. The stranger pressed his forehead with his hands as if trying to dig out some old, very old memory. He continued in his quivering voice. "Let me, let me confess, too! My sins are beginning to emerge from my ruined life like columns under a house that has collapsed. I have also sinned. And how gravely!"

There was silence in the tent. The stranger composed himself and sat down. Quietly and broodingly, as if he began to remember the words that were leaving his lips one by one, he looked into the candlelight and began to talk. "A long time ago, if I remember well, I had a small mirror. It was a small, unpretentious, plain mirror. My father gave it to me when I was about to set out on a long journey—my father, may his memory be blessed. And, my brothers, I forgot my father and his name; I forgot everything, and I forgot the mirror too. One time, much later, when I had already left everything behind—my religion, my past—I was sitting with my fiancée in our garden on a fine summer evening. I leaned my head on her shoulder, inhaling the fragrance of her hair, her beautiful, golden hair. And we were laughing in our happiness. Suddenly, my fiancée's blond hair, which was like a golden sea, became loose. Clarissa's hair—"

There was deadly silence in the tent. The stranger went on talking, nearly out of breath, "Yes, her name was Clarissa. She wasn't a Jewish woman, my brothers. She blushed and burst out laughing, and asked me for a mirror so that she might put her hair back in order. My brothers, I looked and searched, and behold! I found a mirror in my pocket. *That* mirror. My father's mirror. How did it get there after so many years? Who sent it there so it would get into my hand? I don't know. Fate played a trick on me. As I was about to hand it to my lover, I looked into it and I got frightened. My father's face appeared in the mirror, my father whom I had forgotten or wanted to forget, but whose face I no longer knew. It was his kind, old face that looked at me sadly, reproachingly, and mournfully. My father's face. It was like a painting. Or a message, a warning. I looked at Clarissa, her shining, blond beauty. Suddenly my heart was filled with wild anger. I was angry at my father. Why did he appear just then? Why did he want to separate me from her, from love? I tried to cloud the mirror with my breath. But it didn't work. The picture remained there, growing sharper and more frightening: my father! He wouldn't leave. Then I said, 'Clarissa, I want to wipe everything off that mirror so that only you will be in it, only you will be seen in it, your beauty, forever. If the mirror shows faces only, let it show you and not that—old Jew.' That's what I said. Then I started to rub the mirror with rose petals until my father's image disppeared from it and I gave it to my fiancée. From then on her beauty filled up the mirror, her blond hair and her forget-me-not-blue eyes. We were happy and loved each other on that summer evening."

The stranger threw himself on the table. He had to pause. Then he raised his head, and went on talking, hesitantly as if he were dreaming.

"One day, three years later—yes, our son, our only son, was already two years old—the nurse ran desperately out of the garden. The little boy, who had been playing there had found a mirror. Perhaps it was *that* mirror, my brothers. I am sure it was *that* mirror, and he played with it, making it reflect the sun's image. And the bright summer sun that was shining with all of its strength upon the mirror suddenly reflected into the child's eyes. Those little eyes could not endure the brightness that struck them. It was the sun, the sun that had got into the mirror, and the child's eyes became inflamed. A week later he went blind."

The stranger relapsed into silence. He looked into the flames. Reb Chayyim Szüszmann cried out, "I understand. The sin was terrible and the punishment was terrible. God took away a child's eyes for the father's sin."

The stranger remained motionless. "The child's eyes," he said quietly, "yes, for the father's sin. It's been twenty years. But if the father amends his ways, confesses his sin, and wants to atone for it, who will give back the child his eyesight?"

There was commotion around the table. A Jew was elbowing his way to the fore. "That's no way for a Jew to talk, stranger," he shouted. "You must not have doubts. God makes wonders whenever He wills. If a sinner amends his ways and atones for his sins, God will help him in his eternal mercy. Your son may recover. There are similar cases elsewhere. Didn't you read in the papers what happened today right here in Debrecen? A landowner's wife brought her blind son here to have him examined by a doctor from Pest who was visiting in the city. And the doctor cured him and gave back his eyesight by performing an operation in one minute. You see, you must not lose faith and hope."

The stranger raised his head. "Here, in Debrecen?" he asked. "Who was that blind boy? Who was he?"

The Jew shrugged his shoulders, "The child of some landowner from Szabolcs county. His name is Kállay, I believe."

The stranger looked at him. "Kállay?"

"Kállay, of course, a Kállay," the Jew smiled. "There are enough of them around. Here, read the paper—*Az Ellenőr*."[22]

He gave him the newspaper. The stranger stared at it.

Trembling in his whole body, he raised himself from the table. "My brothers," he said quietly, "did you say that

God's mercy will be upon the atoning sinner? What can I do, what can I do to be deserving of God? To show that I shall return to Him on this day? My sin is graver than the sins of others. I must atone for it longer than others. I have suffered, cried, fasted, and wandered a great deal. But I feel all of that was not sufficient. I believe that there is only one kind of redemption for me, the great redemption—death. But death with God's blessing, the death that Jews die—with resignation, tranquillity, and love toward God, death among Israel's dead. That's the way I'd like to redeem myself and that's the way I want to return to God."

Some of the faithful stood up in the tent and pressed closer to the stranger. An uncertain, dim light appeared on the leaf-covered roof. The dawn was breaking. The dawn of *Hoshano Rabbo,* the day of divine help. Reb Chayyim Szüszmann looked at the stranger and said, "Redemption? We cannot impose upon you compulsory attendance at services. Perhaps you cannot even pray. If you are seeking death, may it be according to your wish. We need a pious grave-digger in our small cemetery at the edge of the city. Do you want to be the servant of death?"

The stranger bowed his head, "Yes."

"We've got an old man out there," the rabbi continued. "He keeps the house of mourning in order and takes care of the graves. You will be his helper. If you are looking for death, your wish will be fulfilled. You will give the last respects to the Jewish dead, that will be your redemption. To raise a mound over the pious—that will be your redemption. And you may dig your own grave, a Jewish grave, *kever Yisroel,* and sit by it alone, day after day, out in the cemetery preparing for death, purification, and coming home; and that will be your redemption. What is your name?"

"I am Reb Mayer," the stranger raised his head. "I don't know my other name."

The rabbi nodded, "You're hired, Reb Mayer. Would

you like to go to the cemetery, among the graves, at dawn? Then accompany him, Reb Dovid and Reb Gershom! Go now, the morning is near."

The stranger bowed. He shook hands with everyone in the room. He walked to the deserted street, limping and leaning on the two who accompanied him.

They crossed the main square. Suddenly they reached a large building. There was light in some of its windows. Mayerl stopped. "What's that?" he asked. "The Golden Bull Hotel," replied Reb Dovid, coughing in the cool autumn air.

Mayerl just stood in front of the hotel. His heart started to beat faster. Suddenly, he noticed a shadow up on the second floor. Someone was leaning out of the window in that early morning hour, someone who could not sleep, someone who was keeping vigil.

Reb Gershom coughed again and urged them to go on. The cemetery was still far off. But Mayerl did not move; he kept watching the window. He recognized the shadow up there beyond the curtain.

It was true—it was. His wife and son were in Debrecen. They came to the doctor. They must have searched for him. They would probably go to the county authorities, to the subprefect, to the gendarmes, just as they had been doing for half a year since he disappeared. There they were, up there, a few feet away—his whole past. Clarissa and his son who could see again. And he, the father, down in the street, like a beggar, miserable and deserted, on his way to the cemetery.

He felt like those condemned to death. He knew that it was his last journey. There was no return from where he was going. A day or two, perhaps a week, and he would be resting forever in a grave that he had dug. From there he would never return.

Up there the shadow moved. The curtain fluttered, it seemed. Mayerl sighed. "God is great," he murmured. And a teardrop rolled down his wrinkled cheek. Then he leaned on his cane and they started walking toward the cemetery. The excitement slowly subsided in the tent. The men returned to their seats and stared into the candlelight, leaning against one another in the cool air of the dawn. Reb Chayyim Szüszmann took off his glasses and turned toward them. "The child, my brother, the child! That's our most important task. You saw it, you heard it. Children must be watched so that they remain pure and sinless. The father must be careful that his child will not suffer for his sins. He must be protected from strange fire, strange women, and their beauty. Nothing good will ever come of it. How happy that man has been with a strange woman, and you saw how he went toward his grave. That should be the lesson—Jewish life, Jewish morals, Jewish purity. Then your children will be beautiful, healthy, and happy. And do you know, my brothers, that the children save us in the hour of danger? The children guide us back from turmoil and destruction. Let me tell you an instructive story that the zaddik of Kálló, Reb Eizik Taub, used to tell to children on the eve of Kol Nidre."[23]

The men huddled closer together. And the rabbi in the small tent started to speak in a voice that became quieter and sadder as he went on, until the legend faded into the morning stillness. "You know, on the eve of Kol Nidre, the zaddik of Kálló, may his memory be blessed, gathered the children around him in front of the Ark of the Covenant. And he said to them, 'My dear children, *yalde koydesh bachure chemed,* dear little nurslings, I am going to tell you a tale about how God will forgive us for our sins because of you. Once upon a time there was a father who went on a long journey with his son. Whenever they came to a river, a valley gaping under their feet, or a rock blocking their path, the father lifted his son upon his shoulders and crossed the obstacles. Once, however, after sundown, they came to a large, dreary castle. The heavy iron gate in the wall of the castle was closed. Only the windows, small, narrow windows were open. And the father said to his son, "I have carried you with love and patience, but I have come to the end of my strength. There is a great obstacle lying in front of us. That large gate will not open for me. But those small windows in the wall are open. You can get into the castle by climbing through them and open the gate for me. You will have to help me, my son." That is why I am speaking to you now, my children. We, the fathers, struggle for you, exert ourselves on your behalf, and carry you upon our shoulders throughout the year. But now, when we are standing in front of the great Court, the Gate of Heaven is closed. Our sinful prayers cannot enter it because we are old, tired, and exhausted. O children pray for us! Let our prayers, like so many lively birds, rise, and among them your prayers will reach Heaven because you are small and innocent. Go, children, open the gate for us. That large, heavenly gate, the Gate of Mercy, the Gate of Love, so that redemption may come upon Judah, happiness and peace upon Israel. Amen. Amen.' "

11

The Zaddik Marks Off His Resting Place

When the zaddik of Kálló felt his death approaching he called for the officials of the *Chevra Kaddisha*.[1] "My dear sons, accompany me to the cemetery. I would like to look around there for a while."

The small group set out toward the cemetery. The officials walked along silently. Their souls were weighed down by painful foreboding. The zaddik himself seemed somewhat tired; from his eyes, however, the light of perpetual life radiated. With his customary kind smile on his lips, he turned to everyone he met. "This road is the road of returning home," he observed quietly. "But should the child returning home from the harsh, unknown world be mourned?"

They arrived. As they entered the gate, the rebbe stopped and glanced around. "How many graves, how many liberated lives! Perhaps there is not even room for me here."

A small bird, sitting on a high tree next to him, started singing. It was like an answer to a question. The zaddik lifted his eyes to the tiny singer, "Yes—yes—the light of eternal life is in you, too; in the branch upon which you are standing; in the blades of grass that even the slightest breeze can stir into motion; and in the worms that are carelessly crushed by human feet."

The rebbe walked on. The little bird followed them, flying back and forth. The zaddik's smiling eyes followed the course of its flight. Then he stopped at a tree next to the gate of the cemetery. The little bird was already there. It fluttered nervously from branch to branch. The rebbe meditated for a moment. "We shall mark off my grave here, my sons," he said. "I shall be the last one to be buried here. Lay those who shall follow me in the new cemetery."

12

The Zaddik's Tombstone

In the last moments, the zaddik sent for his most trusted disciples. "You shall not inscribe words of praise upon my tombstone. I have never liked flattery. The marble slab should only tell the onlooker that I was a simple and honest Jew who studied the Law and taught the people truth and love."

And so it happened. In the leap year of 1821/5581, on the seventh day of the Second Adar, the zaddik died. He was seventy years old. He had been Chief Rabbi of Szabolcs county for forty years. The brief inscription on his tombstone lives up to the last wish of the great spirit. The last line in particular moved the soul. They were simple, reflective words: "He could study and was an honest Jew."

Notes

1 *The Rebbe's Song*

1. Soldiers of Ferenc Rákóczi, II, during the Revolt of 1703–1711.
2. Yiddish: "my teacher," a rabbi.

2 *The Singing Saint*

1. A city in southeastern Poland.
2. Passover.
3. Feast of Esther.
4. Hebrew: "unleavened bread."
5. Hebrew: "a collection (of water)," a ritual bath.
6. Hebrew: "order," feast and religious service on the first and second evenings of Passover.
7. Hebrew: "telling," the narrative containing benedictions, prayers, and psalms and recited at the Seder on the eve of Passover.

4 *Moshiach ben David and the Prophet Elijah in Kálló*

1. The eve of Passover.

6 *Forget-Me-Not*

1. The Day of Atonement.
2. Additional prayer recited on the Sabbath and the festivals.
3. Yiddish: "Poor me! What is going to become of us?"
4. Yiddish: "Gentlemen," i.e., "My friends."
5. Hebrew: "the Angel of Evil."
6. Hebrew: "a tabernacle."
7. The name of the ninth month of the Jewish year. Chanukkah, the Festival of Lights, begins on the twenty-fifth day of Kislev.
8. An educated aristocrat whose library contained thousands of French

190

Notes

191

books banned by the strict censorship under Empress Maria Theresa, Count Mihály Sztáray was one of the first important representatives of the Enlightenment in Hungary and a disciple of Voltaire.
9. Town south of Nagykálló.
10. The longest river in Hungary. It flows across Szabolcs county. It is often called the "true Magyar" river, because its course, unlike that of the Danube, does not leave the territory of the country.
11. Hungarian currency before 1945.
12. Yiddish: "the wife of a rabbi."
13. Yiddish: "With your permission," i.e., "May the blessing of the Lord be upon you."
14. Towns north of Nagykálló.
15. Town east of Nagykálló.
16. Town north of Nagykálló.
17. Nagyhalász, town north of Nagykálló.
18. Tiszabercel, town north of Nagykálló.
19. Tiszakarád, town north of Nagykálló.
20. Town northwest of Nagykálló.
21. Town northwest of Nagykálló.
22. The second largest city in Hungary.
23. "My son, walk not thou in the way with them, Restrain thy foot from their path." (Proverbs 1:15)
24. Slow movement.
25. Moderately slow, sorrowful movement.
26. Fast, lively movement.
27. Yiddish: "a nobleman."
28. County north of Szabolcs county.
29. Yiddish: "a cantor."
30. Town north of Nagykálló.
31. Nyirtass, town north of Nagykálló.
32. Members of local aristocracy.
33. District in northeastern Hungary.
34. German: "anniversary," i.e., the anniversary of someone's death.
35. Hebrew: "Merciful God, remove the yoke from our necks."
36. Yiddish: "You must trust, always trust, forever trust God."
37. Hebrew: "sufferings."
38. Hebrew: "morning," the morning prayer.
39. Hungarian sheep dogs.
40. Yiddish: "Mózsi, you are drunk again!"
41. Hebrew: "a document of divorce."
42. The third largest city in Hungary.
43. Leader of the Hungarian Jacobins. He was executed on May 20, 1795.
44. Kazinczy (1759–1831) was one of the fathers of modern Hungarian literature and the "guardian" of the Hungarian language.

45. Ferenc Szentmarjay (1767–1795), one of the members of the Martinovics group, was executed on May 20, 1795.
46. Town south of Nagykálló.
47. Ófehértó, town east of Nagykálló.
48. Town north of Nagykálló.
49. Yiddish: "My father."
50. Hebrew: "The prophet Elijah! The prophet Elijah!"
51. Nyirtura, town north of Nagykálló.

7 *The Market of Debrecen*

1. Town west of Nagykálló.
2. Town northwest of Nagykálló.
3. Town southwest of Nagykálló.
4. Sátoraljaújhely, city in northeastern Hungary.
5. Today the Rumanian city of Oradea.
6. Yiddish: "an attendant," the salaried sexton in a synagogue.
7. German silver coin.
8. Town south of Nagykálló.
9. Probably Ujfehértó; see n3 above.

8 *The Wedding of Levelek*

1. Town north of Nagykálló.
2. Hebrew: "room," i.e., an old-fashioned, private elementary school run by a teacher (rebbe).
3. Polish: "a saucer," i.e., the wide-rimmed hat worn by the hasidim.
4. Hebrew: "a frivolous person," also the sarcastic elf in Jewish folklore.
5. Hebrew: "the shaking of hands," i.e., an unwritten agreement.
6. Hebrew: "a betrothal document," a list of specific premarriage conditions and arrangements.
7. Itinerant Jewish folk musicians.
8. Towns near Nagykálló.
9. Town north of Nagykálló.
10. Jesters at Jewish weddings.
11. Counties in northeastern Hungary.
12. Hebrew: "covering," a canopy under which the wedding ceremony is performed.
13. Yiddish: "the singing of the bridegroom."
14. Yiddish: "Listen, my dear bridegroom, may God keep you in happiness and rejoicing."
15. Yiddish: "the singing of the bride."
16. "Incline your ears to the words of my mouth." (Psalm 78:1)
17. Hungarian: "Phooey."

18. Yiddish: "the bridegroom's side," i.e., the bridegroom's relatives.
19. Yiddish: "the bride's side," i.e., the bride's relatives.
20. Yiddish: "a brief biblical or talmudic discourse."
21. Yiddish: "a wedding gift."
22. Yiddish: "an unmarried young man," usually a yeshivah student.
23. Hebrew: "He who shows mercy to the world."
24. Hebrew: "He who shows mercy to the creatures."
25. Hebrew: "that which is written," i.e., a marriage document or contract.
26. Hebrew: "Our God, make sorrow, sadness, anger, and pain disappear. Bless us with happiness so that even the speechless may sing Your praise."
27. Portuguese: "Act of Faith," the ceremony of pronouncing a judicial verdict of the Inquisition.
28. The square of burning.
29. Hebrew: "a repentant sinner."
30. Aramaic: ."holy," the prayer recited at the conclusion of certain parts of the prayer service. It is a hymn in praise of God and for the coming of the Messiah.
31. The name of the third month of the Jewish year.

9 *The Three Card Players*

1. Weekly portion, Exodus 18–20.
2. Hebrew: "sanctification," a prayer recited on the eve of the Sabbath and the festivals.
3. Hebrew: "songs," sung during and after meals on the Sabbath.
4. Sárospatak, city north of Nagykálló.
5. City in southern Moravia (Czechoslovakia).
6. City west of Nagykálló.
7. The Sabbath loaf.
8. City northwest of Nagykálló.
9. Villages near Nagykálló.
10. Yiddish: "Once the Rebbe crossed the sea . . ."
11. Yiddish: "Once the Rebbe crossed the sea
    The Rebbe, Reb Meir the wonder-worker,
    And what would take someone a hundred years
    It took him a minute.
    And when the Rebbe is on the road
    His hasids travel with him, of course."
12. Yiddish: "But the unbelievers, the empty doubters do not believe a word of this."
13. An important person; usually the head of a talmudic academy or the leader of a Jewish community.
14. Name of a steppe west of Debrecen in northeastern Hungary.

15. Formerly Máramarossziget in the northeastern county of Máramaros. Today the Rumanian city of Sighet.

10 *Mayerl*

1. Formerly a Hungarian city in the county of the same name. Today the Czechoslovakian city of Bratislava.
2. Known from the initials of his name, Rabbi Shlomo (Solomon) b. Isaac (1040–1105) was the greatest of talmudic commentators and biblical exegetes.
3. Yiddish: "Rashi asks," the accustomed question initiating an explanation of or a commentary on a difficult talmudic or biblical passage.
4. Nagyvárad. Today the Rumanian city of Oradea.
5. Town northwest of Nagykálló.
6. Town northwest of Nagykálló.
7. Probably Nyirtelek, town between Tiszalök and Nyiregyháza.
8. Tiszaeszlár, town northwest of Nagykálló, was the scene of a famous ritual murder trial in 1882–83.
9. Starting on the eve of the ninth day of the month of Av, Jews commemorate the anniversary of the destruction of Jerusalem by fasting from sunset to sunset.
10. Tiszanagyfalú, town north of Tiszaeszlár.
11. Members of local aristocracy.
12. Wine grown on sandy soil.
13. Formerly Hungarian city in the northwestern county of Máramaros. Today in the Soviet Union.
14. Hebrew: "a young branch of a tree," especially a palm branch used on the Feast of Tabernacles (*Sukkos*).
15. See *Forget-Me-Not,* n6, above.
16. Hebrew: "the great *hoshana*," the name of the seventh and concluding day of the Feast of Tabernacles (*Sukkos*).
17. Town southwest of Debrecen.
18. Hebrew: "Pentateuch," the first five books of Moses.
19. Yiddish: "Who are you, Jew?"
20. Yiddish: "Don't you know Hebrew "
21. Hebrew: "I remember my transgressions."
22. *The Inspector,* a Hungarian newspaper.
23. Hebrew: "all vows," the prayer that ushers in the Day of Atonement.

11 *The Zaddik Marks Off His Resting Place*

1. Hebrew: "Holy Brotherhood," the community organization among the Ashkenazi Jews responsible for the burial of the dead in accordance with traditional custom.

Bibliography

Neumann, Albert. *Történetek a "Kállói Cádik"—ról (Stories about the Zaddik of Kálló)*. Nyiregyháza, 1935.

Patai, Jósef. *"A Nótás szent"* ("The Singing Saint"). *Mult és Jövő* (April 1917).

Szabolcsi, Lajos. *Délibáb (Zsidó legendáskönyv (Mirage [A Book of Jewish Legends])*. Budapest, 1927.

195